SEALED *with a* KISS

LOREE LOUGH

W
WHITAKER
HOUSE

SEALED WITH A KISS
(Also included in *Prevailing Love: 3-in-1 Collection*)

Loree Lough
www.loreelough.com

ISBN: 978-1-60374-578-9
Printed in the United States of America
© 1999, 2010 by Loree Lough

Whitaker House
1030 Hunt Valley Circle
New Kensington, PA 15068
www.whitakerhouse.com

This book has been printed digitally and produced in a standard specification in order to ensure its continuing availability.

Dedication

First, to my faithful readers, whose support and faith keep me writing.

Second, to Larry, light of my life and stirrer
of my soul, for whom I'm happy to obey
1 Corinthians 7:10: "Let not the wife depart from her husband."

Special mention to my wonderful editor,
Courtney, and the ever-capable Lois.

Finally, to my once abused, now spoiled dog, who put aside his Frisbee
addiction long enough for me to write these stories!

Prologue

May 31, 2009
London, England

S am Sylvester was dying, and he knew it.

When he closed his eyes, he could picture the huge red truck careening around the corner on two wheels, its chrome bumper aiming straight for the convertible's windshield.

Right before the impact, he'd glanced at Shari. As usual when they were driving, she'd had her nose buried in the pages of a romance novel. "It helps keep my mind off all the dangerous drivers," she'd once said. *It doesn't get any more ironic than that,* Sam thought.

He wondered where Shari was now. He'd seen the paramedics load her, bloodied and unconscious, into one of the ambulances at the scene. Had the Lord, in His infinite mercy, decided to take her home then and there, to spare her any suffering?

It was a struggle just to open his eyes, but Sam forced himself. Nothing in the bustling emergency room could possibly be as horrible as the pictures in his mind.

"Look 'ere, doctor," came the mask-muffled Cockney accent of a nurse. "'e seems to be coming round."

The broad, beefy face of a doctor peered at Sam from behind a surgical mask. "You know where you are, sir?" he asked, bushy brows drawn together in a frown.

Under other circumstances, Sam might have chuckled, because the doctor's breath was causing the pleats of his white mask to puff in and out like the bellows of a tiny accordion. Instead, Sam tried to muster the strength to nod. Yes, he knew exactly where he was—on his way to heaven.

But you can't go, he told himself. *At least not yet.* There was so much to do, so much to say, so many questions to ask before—

"M-my wife...." The words scraped from his parched throat like sandpaper across roughened wood. "W-where's my wi—?"

"Down the hall," said the nurse, patting his hand.

"Is she...is she—?"

The expression on her face told him everything he needed to know. Shari had already joined their Maker in Paradise. But maybe, just maybe, he'd read the blue eyes above the mask wrong....

He ignored the pain—pain that seemed to have no particular source, throbbing in every joint and every muscle. He screwed up his courage. He had to know for sure before he let go of this earthly life.

"Did she make it?"

In the moment of hesitation and silence that followed his question, Sam felt his own lifeblood seeping slowly onto the gurney beneath him. The doctors and nurses surrounding him were all perspiring, so why, he wondered, did he feel so *cold?*

Drowsiness threatened to take him far, far from the ER, but he fought it. "Did she make it?" he repeated with force.

"No, Mr. Sylvester," said the whisper-soft voice of the nurse, "I'm afraid she didn't." Another gentle pat. "But I can promise y' this—she didn't suffer."

Sam closed his eyes as a curious mix of gratitude and regret propelled a slow, groaning breath past his lips. Gratitude that his precious wife wouldn't be "up there" alone for long. Regret because their sweet little girl would have to live the rest of her days without them.

At least Molly will have Ethan, thank God.

Ethan...every bit as alone in the world as Molly would soon be.

For the first time since he'd regained consciousness, Sam felt a profound fear pulse through him. *Ethan.... They need to contact him right now because Molly's going to need him!*

With a strength that belied his condition, he gripped the nurse's wrist. "What...what did they do with...where are my things?" he choked out.

"In a locker, just down the hall." She fished in the pocket of her surgical gown as the corners of her eyes crinkled with a sympathetic smile. "I 'aven't 'ad a chance yet to file it," she said, withdrawing a key.

The way it caught and reflected the light made it look like a silvery cross, if only for an instant. In that instant, Sam pictured Jesus welcoming Shari home. "In my wallet," he said, struggling for air now, "there's a business card, and—"

Her blonde brows knitted with concern. "Please calm yourself, Mr. Sylvester."

"Why?"

He watched as she blinked and tried to come up with a rational reason for him to calm down. His mind started to wander, and he recalled how he'd been a volunteer EMT in Maryland before moving to London. He'd witnessed enough accident scenes to know what impending death looked like. He knew that the remainder of his life could be numbered in minutes, and that he had just one reason to conserve his remaining strength: Molly.

He thought about the joy she'd brought into his life, into Shari's. From the moment they'd picked up their round-faced infant at that crowded Korean orphanage eleven years ago, she'd enchanted them with her dancing brown eyes and elfin smile. And the first thing every morning since, Sam and Shari had thanked the Almighty for blessing them with their beautiful, raven-haired angel.

Life from now on would be hard for her. Very hard, especially at first. But Molly knew the Lord, and He would help her through those first sorrow-filled days. And she'd have her uncle Ethan to look out for her.

Molly adored Ethan, and Ethan had always loved Molly as much as if she were his own. Sam and Shari had discussed it dozens of times. The way he looked at Molly, the tenderness in his voice when he spoke to her—*that* was the reason they'd decided to make him godfather *and* guardian to their only child.

This would be hard for Ethan, too, Sam knew. But he'd be a good father to Molly. Sam was as certain of that as he was of God's boundless love.

From out of nowhere, a line Sam had read somewhere reverberated in his head: *In knowledge, there is power.* Knowing Molly would be in good hands gave him enough physical power to persist with the nurse. "The card," he said again, "will you...get it...for me?"

The doctor nodded his approval, and the nurse left to collect Sam's belongings. He closed his eyes. *Father,* he prayed, *let me hold on a little longer, for Molly's sake....*

"Is this it?"

Squinting, Sam smiled crookedly at the card held between the nurse's thumb and forefinger. "After all that fuss," he croaked out, "I'm ashamed to admit I...to admit that...that I can't focus enough....to read it."

"It says 'Burke Enterprises,' and under that, 'Ethan Burke, President and CEO.'"

A relieved sigh rattled from his lungs. "Praise God," he whispered. "Praise Jesus!"

For a moment, an odd stillness settled over the cramped, brightly lit cubicle, despite the blips and hums of the equipment monitoring his heart rate and pulse, despite the nonstop efforts of the medical team to repair his broken, battered body.

"What's your name?" he asked the nurse.

She raised her eyebrows high on her forehead, her stethoscope bobbing, as she pointed to her chest.

"Yes, you."

"Tricia Turner."

Reaching for her hand, he said, "Will you call him for me, Tricia?" Sam squeezed her hand.

"I'll see it gets done, soon as—"

Another squeeze, tighter this time, interrupted her. "I'd like *you* to do it." Sam spoke slowly, knowing he had to conserve his waning strength until he could be sure Molly would be with Ethan as soon as was humanly possible. "You know as well as I that I'm not walking out of here, Tricia, so say you'll grant me this last wish."

She blinked once, twice, and then said, "I—I'll try."

"No," Sam all but barked. "Promise me, before I die. Because my wife and I chose Ethan, there," Sam said, nodding toward the card, "to be our daughter's guardian, should anything happen to us. She's only eleven, you see, and I—"

"I understand. And you have my word. I'll phone him for you."

"I have your word?"

She nodded just once, but it was enough. A feeling of great peace settled over Sam, and, smiling, he let go of her hand. "Thank you. And bless you, Tricia, for your kindness...for giving me peace."

When she began to fade from view, Sam thought, *Not a good sign. Not good at all.* Good thing he'd given Molly an extra-big hug and an especially big kiss that morning. *Good thing you told her how much you love her. And how you taught her to turn to God in times of trouble.* The girl would need it—soon.

Soon, soon, soon, he chanted in his mind as a drowsy, dizzy sensation wrapped around him. The pain was gone now, and he felt nothing but the feathery weight of the stick-on patches that held the heart monitor wires in place on his chest. Sam closed his eyes and listened to the high-pitched one-note whine of the monitor.

"Code blue!" someone hollered.

"Crash cart, stat!" yelled someone else.

Their shouts didn't startle him. Sam was beyond fear now. Somewhere in the deepest recesses of his conscious mind, he remembered his days as a paramedic, when he'd seen the flat line on the monitor signal the end of a life.

This is the last time you'll have that memory...last memory you'll have, period!

Did the saints in heaven remember their days on earth? And if they did, were they granted permission to visit their former world? Sam hoped so, because he wanted desperately to know that he could look in on Molly from time to time.

The lead surgeon on the team applied electric paddles to Sam's chest, then bellowed "Clear!" as Tricia prepared a syringe for one last-ditch effort to save him. But Sam knew it was pointless. Soon, they'd realize the futility of their efforts, and by the time the doctor called time of death, he'd be with his Father, and with Shari, in Paradise.

Sam said one last prayer:

Lord Jesus, be with Ethan now. Guide his steps and his words, for Molly's sake, as well as for his....

Chapter One

Same day, Potomac Hills, Maryland

There'd been a time when Ethan had enjoyed hosting parties—the bigger, the better—especially right here on his own riverfront estate. But his heart wasn't in this one. Hadn't been "in" much of anything lately.

Not so long ago, his parties had been described in the society pages as "colorful affairs." But there hadn't been much color in his life lately, either. Even the sun setting over the Potomac seemed drab and washed out.

Ethan stood on the pier, hands in his pockets, and looked back toward the great expanse of lawn, where no fewer than a hundred well-dressed guests meandered from tennis court to swimming pool to dual-level deck.

You've got it all, he thought, frowning. And from all outward appearances, he did have it all—a successful, self-made business; a big, beautiful house on three acres of prime Maryland real estate; seven automobiles—a sleek, high-priced sports car (for impressing the ladies), a classy, imported sedan (for impressing clients), and five roadsters of various vintages to impress himself...and neighbors who were rich and famous, to boot.

So why did he feel like something was missing? Something meaningful, something *vital*?

There were two bright spots in Ethan's life: Burke Enterprises and his Korean-born goddaughter, Molly. The mere thought of the pretty preteen raised his spirits a bit. In another couple of weeks, Molly and her parents would arrive for a long, leisurely vacation, and already, he was counting down the days until the family would leave London for their annual trek to Maryland.

A woman's shrill voice broke into his thoughts. "Peewee-than!" she hollered. "*There you are!*"

It was Kate, the six-foot, blonde marketing manager his vice president had appointed a couple months back. She waved a hand of red-taloned fingers above her head, and he sent a halfhearted salute in return, then faced the slow-surging river and ran both hands through his hair. He'd been neatly dodging her blatant flirtations all afternoon, pretending the ice bucket needed to be refilled or feigning a must-have conversation with someone across the way. But now he felt trapped, like a captive standing at the end of the gangplank on a buccaneer ship.

Her high-heeled sandals clickity-clacked as she pranced across the wide, weathered boards of the pier. "Ethan, what are you doing over here all by yourself? People are looking for you."

Of course they were. And why wouldn't they be? Somebody, somewhere, was always seeking him out for any one of a hundred reasons—a favor, a raise, a piece of advice, an introduction to another mover and shaker. With shoulders slumped, he shook his head. *Quit feeling sorry for yourself, pal*, he chided. As his mother would have pointed out, God had blessed him with a lot—materially and otherwise. *But He's taken away a lot, too....*

"Ethan?"

You've got two choices, m'friend, he told himself, grinning slightly as he looked at the water swirling darkly around the pilings. *Jump, or pretend you're pleased to see her.*

Turning, Ethan took a deep breath and fixed a practiced smile on his face. "Kate, darling," he said smoothly, taking the goblet of iced tea from her hand, "looks like you need a refill. Let me get—"

Laughing lightly, she patted her flat stomach. "Please," she gasped, "one more ounce of *anything* and I'll positively pop!"

There was an awkward pause, and Ethan knew she was waiting for him to fill the void with some form of flattery about her figure. Unable to think of a single truthful thing to say, he let the moment pass.

A quick glance at his Rolex told him it was nearly four in the afternoon. Another hour or so and the party would be over. The crowd had already thinned considerably; once the last of them had gone, he'd call Sam and Shari to see if they'd made their airline reservations yet. Last time they'd talked, he'd promised to have a car pick them up at Baltimore-Washington International Airport. They were the closest thing to a family he'd likely ever have, so nothing but the best for them!

Kate linked her arm through his and led him back toward the house. "It sure was nice of you to throw a Memorial Day barbecue for Burke employees and their families," she purred. "I want you to know...I'm *especially* happy to be here."

Yeah, I'll just bet you are, he thought.

His vice president, Pete Maxon, had told Ethan what he'd overheard Kate say two days prior: "If I play my cards right," she told the gaggle of gals gathered near the water cooler, "I'll be Mrs. Ethan Burke by this time next year!"

Mrs. Burke, my foot! "Couldn't very well invite everyone else and leave your name off the guest list, now, could I?" was his bland reply.

By the time Sam and Shari had made him guardian of their only daughter six years earlier, Ethan had pretty much accepted the idea that Molly was the closest he'd come to having a child. He would have loved kids—a house full of them—but a man needed a wife for that. And every female he'd met so far had been like Kate, keeping her tummy flat and her sights firmly fixed on his checkbook. Hardly mother material!

"You look very handsome today," she said, then threw back her back and laughed. "Which isn't to say you don't *always* look handsome. I just meant that in those jeans and that white shirt—"

A gale of robust laughter interrupted her. "Ethan, m'boy! *There* you are! Seems I've walked every inch of this plantation you call a home looking for you." The silver-haired gentleman fixed his gaze on Kate. "Well, now, no wonder I couldn't find him," he told her, wiggling his eyebrows. Leaning in close, he lowered his voice to add, "I'd make myself scarce, too, if my date was as lovely as you."

Ethan heard the phone ringing in the distance. Without knowing why, he tensed. Everyone who might have a reason to call him at home had been invited to the cookout. "Kate isn't my date, Dad," he said distractedly. "She's—"

"Dad?" Kate interrupted. "This attractive young fellow is your father?" She flung an arm over his shoulders. "Why, you don't look nearly old enough to have a son Ethan's age," she cooed.

The older man attempted a W. C. Fields imitation. "My dear, you're an outrageous flirt!"

Kate kept her eyes on Ethan's father. "Now I see where you get your good looks *and* your charm, Ethan." She turned slightly, aiming a haughty expression at her boss. "We-e-e-ell?"

His stiff-backed stance and tight-lipped expression spoke volumes. At least they should have. Kate didn't seem to notice at all how much her presence irked him.

"Aren't you going to introduce us?"

Poor Kate, he thought. *She somehow got the idea that Dad has more money than Donald Trump.* Shoving both hands into his pockets, he stared at the close-cropped lawn in an attempt to hide his grin. *If this is going where I think it's going, you two deserve each other.* "Dad, this is Kate Winslow," came his bored monotone. "Kate, meet Sawyer Burke."

During the introductions, he noticed that the phone had stopped ringing, and he wondered if Maria had answered it or if the machine had taken the call. Wondered, too, why a sense of foreboding still churned in his gut.

"It's a pleasure to make your acquaintance, my dear," Sawyer said, bowing.

Her hands clasped beneath her chin, Kate giggled like a silly schoolgirl. "Oh, but the pleasure is all—"

"Meester Burke! Meester Burke!"

All heads turned toward the deck, where Ethan's housekeeper was leaning over the railing with a portable phone pressed to her aproned bosom. "Hurry," she yelled, waving him closer. *"Muy importante!"*

Maria had worked for Ethan for years. The only other time he'd heard her carry on that way had been last Christmas, when the warmth of the fire had brought hundreds of praying mantis nymphs to life in the branches of the twenty-foot Douglas fir that dominated the living room. His heart pounding with fear and dread, Ethan took the steps two at a time.

There were tears in the eyes of the plump, gray-haired woman when she said, "Oh, Meester Burke…poor leetle Molly…."

Not Molly, Lord, he prayed silently. *Please don't let anything have happened to my sweet Molly….*

With a trembling hand, he accepted the phone and slowly brought it to his ear. "Ethan Burke here…."

"Mr. Burke? Um, my name is, ah, Tricia Turner, and I'm a nurse at 'ampton 'ospital in London? I, uh, well...."

He had a yard full of guests, so why was the little Brit hemming and hawing? But the instant she finished her sentence, Ethan wished he'd never rushed her, even in his mind. Because not even her crisp Cockney accent made it easy to listen to the rapid-fire dispensation of information that followed. Sam and Shari had been killed in a car crash at Trafalgar Square, and their daughter was home alone with her nanny.

"She hasn't been told yet?"

The long pause made him wonder if they'd been disconnected. But then she said, "No. Before Mr. Sylvester passed on, he told us you're the child's guardian. He said you'd take care of everything, including breaking the news about her mum and dad." Another unbearable pause ensued before she added, "'e was one brave chap, that pal of yours, 'oldin' on till 'e knew 'is li'le one would be in good 'ands...."

Ethan slumped into the nearest deck chair, one hand in his hair, the other gripping the phone so tightly his fingers ached. The nurse's tone of voice rather than her words themselves told Ethan that Sam had suffered in the end. *But how like him to bite the bullet until all the loose ends were tied up.*

Suddenly, the full impact of the news hit him. Sam and Shari, gone? Ethan struggled to come to grips with the stunning reality—the finality—of it.

"Mr. Burke? Are y'there?"

The oh-so-British voice snapped him back to attention. "Yes. Yes, sorry."

"'ow long d'you suppose it'll take you to get 'ere? I don't mean to be crass, but there's the matter of...of...."

"Identifying the bodies?"

"Yes. Rules, y'know."

The bodies. The funeral arrangements. Ethan was at a loss for words.

"So you'll be 'ere soon, then…?"

Ethan hung his head, shading his eyes with his free hand. Sam and Shari had trusted him to do what needed to be done should anything like this ever happen. Of course, he hadn't expected there would ever be a need for him to follow through; they'd always been so full of vim and vigor, always so *alive*.

The word reverberated painfully in his brain. If he'd known, when he'd signed the documents making him executor of their estate, that the prospect of making those hard, under-pressure decisions would turn his blood to ice, he might have suggested they hire a lawyer instead. An outsider. Someone who didn't *love* them.

"How soon d'you think you can be 'ere, sir?"

A mental image of Molly, alone in the Sylvesters' London flat with some barely-out-of-her-teens nanny, flashed through his head. She needed him, and if he had to pull every favor owed him, if he had to charter a private jet, he'd get there by morning. "I'll be on the next London-bound plane leaving Baltimore," he said. And, thanking her, Ethan hung up.

Propping the phone on the arm of the deck chair, he stared out at the Potomac. It wouldn't be easy filling Sam's shoes. The guy had made fatherhood look as natural as breathing. No matter how tired or overworked he had been, Sam had always dug deep and found the energy to spend time with his little girl.

Molly had told Ethan no fewer than a dozen times that he was her favorite grown-up. It was one thing playing part-time uncle. Being a full-time dad was something else entirely.

For that precious child's sake, he hoped he was up to the task.

❦

Three months later

Through the two-way mirror in the waiting room, Ethan watched the therapist working with Molly. Miss Majors had been recommended by Pastor Cummings. Ethan had prayed before making the decision, and he prayed now that it had been the right one.

He'd been at his wit's end wondering how to cope with Molly's sad, stoic silence. Then Maria had suggested he turn to his church for help. He might have thought of it himself, except that church hadn't exactly been at the center of his life for the past few years. If not for Molly's refusal to speak, he might not have started attending again. But he'd had no choice. Her condition was his fault—no ifs, ands, or buts.

His head in his hands, Ethan closed his eyes, unable to watch the child's sorrowful expression a moment longer. He loved her as if she were his own flesh and blood; loved her the way he'd loved his sister Bess, his mother....

Why did it seem that whomever he loved deeply suffered?

With his eyes still squinted shut, he couldn't see into the next room, but he could hear every word thanks to the speaker overhead. The pretty, young counselor was pulling out all the stops. She'd tried everything short of a song and dance act to this point, yet Molly hadn't uttered a syllable.

Ethan slouched on the sofa. He kept his eyes closed and let his mind wander back to that terrible morning in London when he'd broken the tragic news to Molly. Despite the speech he'd practiced over and over during the red-eye flight into Heathrow Airport, he'd messed up big time when the moment finally came.

When he'd arrived at Sam and Shari's, it had been easy to smile as Molly skipped around him in a slowly shrinking circle, clapping her hands and squealing with glee that her uncle Ethan had come to visit. They'd played this welcome game since she had been old enough to stand on her own, and he cherished every giggly moment.

That morning, she'd wrapped her arms around him, just as she'd done a hundred times before...and then stopped. "Mommy and Daddy haven't called...."

Worry and fear were etched on her little face, and even as Ethan had prayed for the right words to erase them, he'd known no such power would be granted him that day.

"They always call," she'd said, looking up into his face. "There must be something wrong...."

He'd perched on the edge of the sofa, invited her to sit down beside him, and then, with one arm resting on her slender shoulders, looked into those dark, trusting eyes...and lost it.

What kind of a man are you? Ethan had demanded of himself as tears coursed down his face. *You're blubbering like a baby.... It's your job to comfort Molly, not the other way around!* He'd never felt more like a heel than during those long, harrowing moments when she'd patted his shoulder, saying, "It'll be okay, Uncle Ethan. Don't cry. Won't you tell me why you're so sad?"

A minute or so later, after his carefully chosen words had been uttered, Ethan realized that in the space of a minute, maybe two, he'd completely destroyed her safe little world.

He hated the old adage that said, "Hindsight is always twenty-twenty." However, looking into her shocked, pained eyes made him understand the truth of it as never before. He'd prayed for a kinder, gentler way to break the news. So, why hadn't God delivered on His "ask, and ye shall receive" promise?

He should have been gentler. Should have eked out the information more slowly. Should have brought in a professional to help deliver the awful, life-changing news....

The ugly memory made him groan aloud and drive his fingers through his hair. The all-business attitude that had kept his nose to the grindstone while building Burke Enterprises had given him the drive and motivation to work until he thought he might drop, watch the market with a shrewd eye, and study his competitors even more closely. "Tell it like it is" had become watchwords—no exceptions. Straight talk had never let him down before, but it had backfired miserably that morning with Molly. He wondered what Miss Majors would say about his pathetic performance as a parent.

Well, at least he'd done *one* thing right—he hadn't gone into detail about the accident. He'd been to the morgue and seen his friends' battered, lifeless bodies. The poor kid sure didn't need the image of *that* in her head for a lifetime!

Ethan didn't think he'd ever forget the way her dark lashes had fluttered as her deep-brown eyes filled with tears. She'd begun to quake, as if each tremor was counting the beats of her breaking heart. "B-but...but they *promised*," she'd whimpered.

"Promised what, sweetheart?"

"That...that they'd never leave me. Th-that they'd be here for me, *forever*." She'd punched the sofa cushion. "They can't be dead. It isn't true! It isn't!"

Not knowing what to say, he'd simply held out his arms, his own eyes filling with tears again as he sent a silent message with one nod of his head: *Yes, it's true.*

For a moment, she'd simply sat, staring. Then she'd thrown herself into his arms, and they'd cried together. Ethan had no idea how much time had passed—minutes? half an hour?—before her rib-racking sobs and shirt-soaking tears subsided. Then, Molly had sat back, dried her eyes with the hem of her plaid skirt, and sucked in a huge gulp of air. "It's my fault," she'd whispered, staring blankly ahead.

She hadn't said a word since.

And now, despite Miss Majors' valiant efforts, Molly sat stiff and straight in the bright-red armchair, ankles crossed and hands folded primly in her lap, staring at some indistinct spot on the floor.

It would feel good, actually, to confess his faults and frailties to this stranger; it would feel equally good when she gave him the tongue-lashing he deserved, not that taking his lumps would change anything.

The counselor stood up and walked over to the two-way mirror, flipped a switch on the wall, and tapped on the glass. Up to this point, Ethan had been able to see and hear everything that was going on in the exam room without being visible to its occupants. But now, Miss Majors and Molly could see and hear him, too. The counselor's beautiful green eyes zeroed in on his, and she smiled softly. "Mr. Burke, I realize Molly's session has ended, but I'm hoping you'll stay a few minutes to talk with me."

Ethan blinked, unnerved by her intense scrutiny. *Here it comes,* he thought, *the dressing-down of your lifetime.* "I—uh, well, sure," he stammered, running a hand through his hair. He had the sudden feeling that this nervous habit betrayed a deep psychological disorder, and she must have read his mind, because Miss Majors tilted her head and raised an eyebrow.

She opened the door in the exam room that led to the waiting room, then walked past him purposefully to her office, tossing Molly's file on the blotter on her desk. He followed and stood in the doorway. "She'll be fine in there," the counselor assured him. "As you can see, Molly is all wrapped up in a book she found on the shelf."

He glanced back into the exam room, where, sure enough, Molly was sitting in that same red chair with an open book in her lap. *How long was I lost in thought?* he wondered. "She hasn't been that interested in anything since I brought her home," he admitted, meeting the therapist's eyes. "How'd you get her to do that?"

"It's my job," she said in the same no-nonsense tone he remembered from the telephone conversations that had led up to this appointment. "Please, make yourself comfortable."

She gestured to an upholstered armchair facing her desk.

As comfortable as a body can get in a contraption like this, he thought, sliding onto its seat. Ethan immediately leaned forward, balanced elbows on knees, and said, "So, can you help her or not?"

Miss Majors was standing behind her chair, her pale pink-painted fingernails drumming on the wood-trimmed headrest. When she smiled, the room brightened. He was taken aback until he realized why her smile looked so different, so special. It wasn't a flirty grin intended to knock him for a loop or a seductive smirk meant to advertise her availability, which were the types he'd grown accustomed to receiving from women of all ages. Her smile was honest, unpretentious. She was offering herself, all right… but on a caring, professional level.

Ethan found his respect for her growing, and he'd opened his mouth to compliment her when she said, "Yes, we can help her. But it'll take time, perhaps a lot of it, to find out why she stopped talking."

Pausing, she plopped into her chair. "And it'll take a major time commitment from you, Mr. Burke."

Her voice was soothing, rhythmic, like the calming sound of the Potomac lapping at the piling that supported his pier. Ethan sat back and crossed his legs, resting an ankle on his knee. "I intend to cooperate in any way I can. Tell me what to do, and it's as good as done."

Miss Majors wrote something in Molly's file, then stood up and walked around to the front of her desk. Perching on one corner, she said, "I'm glad to hear that."

His mind began to wander as she matter-of-factly outlined a course of treatment. *She's not much bigger than most of her clients,* he mused. His gaze shifted from her big, green eyes to the mass of long, carrot-colored curls framing her face, making her look like a cross between Julia Roberts and Pippi Longstocking. And really, what kid wouldn't be attracted to a woman like that?

Earlier, as she'd walked ahead of him into her office, he'd felt like a cartoon character floating along on the delectable scent of flowers and sunshine. The aroma reminded him of the hedgerow behind his childhood home...lilacs? Honeysuckle?

Ethan shifted in his chair, suddenly angry with himself. What sort of person was he, anyway, having thoughts like that about the woman who would help his little Molly escape her self-imposed prison of silence?

"If you're agreeable, I'd like to hold all future sessions at your house," she was saying. "At least, until we make some headway."

It appeared she hadn't noticed how far his mind had wandered from Molly, and after a quick prayer of thanks, he nodded.

"I think she'll benefit from being in familiar surroundings."

"I agree."

Miss Majors lifted her chin a notch and tilted her head slightly as those bright eyes zeroed in on his face. "I think it's important for you to be available for the first few sessions, if at all possible."

"Of course, it's possible," he blurted out. "Nothing is more important than Molly."

"Not even Burke Enterprises?"

He clenched his teeth. Hadn't he just said that Molly came first? What did she mean by that crack, anyway? "Not even Burke Enterprises," he affirmed.

She'd said it to put him to the test. He could see it in her eyes, in the way one eyebrow lifted at his response. He'd used the tactic himself plenty of times during hard business negotiations. And from the looks of her approving smile, he'd passed.

"Good," she said matter-of-factly. She returned to the other side of her desk, sat down, and opened her daily planner. "Three times a week, an hour at a time, for starters," she said, clicking a ballpoint pen into action. And without looking up, Miss Majors added, "Mornings are usually best for the kids."

Most of Ethan's business meetings were scheduled first thing in the morning. But he'd just underscored that nothing was more important than Molly, and he aimed to prove it. Reaching into his suit coat pocket, Ethan slid out his electronic calendar. "Nine o'clock?" he asked, hitting the On button.

The upward curve of her full, pink lips told Ethan she hadn't expected him to agree so quickly.

"I owe you an apology, Mr. Burke."

Confused, he blinked. "What? But…why?"

"For appearing inflexible." She shrugged. "I've been at this long enough to know that people rarely say what they mean. Especially people like you—with plenty of money—who can hire others to do what…."

It seemed to Ethan that she hadn't intended to be quite *that* open and honest. Maybe that would teach her not to judge all her wealthy clients by the abysmal behavior of a few.

"Most parents say they want to help," she continued, "and that they understand therapy will take time, and patience, and cooperation. But what they really want is…for me to perform a miracle. Like I'm equipped with a magic wand that'll fix everything with one quick stroke." She gave another shrug. "It's not an altogether fair tactic, but I'll do anything, say anything, go to any lengths, to help my kids."

Her kids? Was that something all the self-professed child experts said to worried parents? Half a dozen other specialists had said the same thing…and had failed to draw Molly out of her shell.

Still, there was something about Miss Majors that made Ethan believe she could no more look him in the eye and lie than leap from the roof of this three-story building and fly to the parking lot! It made him want to give her a shot, if for no other reason than that time was running out. The longer Molly remained in her wordless world, the harder it would be to coax her out of it.

"You're the expert," he conceded. "So even when it's inconvenient, or difficult, I'll make whatever changes are necessary to help Molly."

With pen poised above her book, she smiled. "Just so we can get things started sooner rather than later, what do you think of my coming to your house at seven tomorrow evening? And when we wrap things up, we can schedule dates and times that work for all of us."

"Sounds like a plan to me." Without knowing it, she'd spared him having to cancel and reschedule tomorrow's early-morning meetings. Ethan got to his feet and extended a hand. She stood up, too, and reached across her desk to shake it. The power of her grip surprised him, especially considering her slight frame. If her ideas about helping Molly were as solid as her handshake, things would right themselves in no time.

Ethan pulled a business card out of his pocket and plucked a pencil from a mug on her desk overflowing with writing implements. "It's tough to find my driveway if you don't know what to look for," he said, sketching a small, crude map on the back of the card, "so this should make it a little easier. Just watch for a gray mailbox."

Accepting the map, she thanked him and, nodding, watched him as he left her office and entered the exam room. He felt her eyes on him as he took the girl by the hand and led her down the hall. If he hadn't glanced over his shoulder as he and Molly were waiting for the elevator, he'd never have seen her wiping tears from her gorgeous green eyes. The sight of it touched something in him, though he couldn't say *what*, couldn't understand *why*. Her reaction should have roused deep concern. After all, weren't therapists supposed to remain aloof and unemotional if they hoped to obtain successful results?

It wasn't like him to let go of a suspicion that quickly, that easily. He'd sealed many deals with nothing more than gut instinct to go on. So no one was more surprised than Ethan when he said a silent prayer asking God to help him figure out if he'd made the right choice for Molly—or if he simply wanted to *believe* he had—because something about the pretty counselor called to something desperately lonely deep within himself....

Chapter Two

The sun had begun to set, reminding Hope of a brassy coin sliding ever so slowly into a slot on the glowing horizon. She rolled down her car window and let the air riffle her curls. But neither she nor the wind could distract her mind from thoughts of Molly Sylvester.

Professional detachment, she'd learned, protected her from letting what she *felt* interfere with what she *knew* was best for her patients. And that mind-set had guided her well so far.

But things seemed different this time.

Very different.

In the four years since she'd become a Christian counselor, Hope had worked with hundreds of troubled children, some barely old enough to walk, others whose teenage years were all but behind them. Some had lost a mom or a dad, and, with prayer and plenty of tender loving care, she'd helped them come to terms with their grief. But Molly had lost both parents at the same time.

The night before, while poring over psychology books and case studies in search of answers to the long list of questions raised by Molly's refusal to speak, Hope couldn't help but wonder if that fact alone explained the close connection she felt to the sad-eyed child.

Lost in her thoughts, Hope missed the Route 270 exit. She'd barely gotten back on track when the map Ethan had drawn fluttered out the window. Now she'd have to pull over to call him and ask him to repeat the directions. Groaning inwardly, she wondered if he'd worry about having made a mistake by putting Molly in the hands of a woman who couldn't even hold on to the map that would help her begin the girl's therapy.

It shouldn't matter what he thought of her. Losing the directions that way—well, it could have happened to anyone. But for a reason she couldn't explain, it mattered. A lot. Hope shifted uncomfortably in the driver's seat, and just as she was about to steer toward the road's shoulder to call him, she spotted a large, round-topped, gray mailbox.

Hadn't Ethan said his mailbox was gray?

She slowed down, instantly noticing BURKE spelled out in bold, black letters. And beneath the name, 435 RIVER VIEW.

Hope pulled into the driveway and headed down the narrow ribbon of blacktop, thanking the Lord as she neared the house for sparing her from having to admit she'd lost the directions. The quickly waning light of day was further dimmed by the thin canopy of trees overhead. Hope's heart began beating in double time. She'd conducted therapy sessions in children's homes before, so she didn't understand why this particular one was making her so nervous.

But you do understand, she chided herself, remembering that after arriving home from work the night before, she'd typed Ethan Burke's name into an Internet search engine. In an eyeblink, a lengthy list had appeared on the screen, and, in no time, she'd found herself skimming photographs and articles of Ethan arm wrestling with Harrison Ford, Ethan posing with Maryland's governor, Ethan munching a hot dog from the bench inside the Orioles' dugout, Ethan at the Kidney Ball, Ethan at the American Heart Association Ball…a different glamorous woman clinging to his tuxedo-jacketed arm at each event.

Next, Hope had read the "Hometown Boy Does Good" story in the magazine section of the *Sunday Sun*. And the *Washington Post* piece that explained how he'd renovated the dilapidated historic manor house on his Potomac River property. She hadn't needed to print out any of the photos to get a clear picture of his lifestyle: Ethan Burke was a self-made millionaire, and, no doubt, a typical spoiled, self-centered bachelor.

A squirrel scampered in front of her car, and Hope braked hard to avoid hitting it. The critter froze when her tires squealed. "Didn't your mama teach you to look both ways before crossing the road?" she gently scolded the rodent as it darted into the thick underbrush alongside the driveway.

Much as she hated to admit it, the near miss had been more her fault than the squirrel's. Her attention had been diverted by imagining what Ethan's house would look like on the inside. She continued down the drive, expecting a stately two-story colonial. White, no doubt, with dozens of multipaned windows and black shutters. Would it feature a semicircular portico? Or huge marble pillars supporting a white-railed balcony? Surely, there'd be a guardhouse, with a red-jacketed servant who'd ask to see Hope's driver's license before allowing her access to Ethan Burke's haven....

Through the trees up ahead, two massive brick columns came into view, each holding up a black, wrought-iron gate. Instead of a sentry on duty, Hope found a stainless steel speaker attached to a black post. She pressed the button marked Talk and waited.

"Can I help you?"

Despite the sputtering and hissing sounds, she recognized the masculine voice in an instant. No wonder he'd so easily wooed the women in those pictures! "Hi, Mr. Burke...Hope Majors, here for my seven o'clock appointment with Molly...."

A second of silence ticked by before his voice cracked through the box again. "Hey there! Just sit tight while I open the gate...."

She gave a haughty little nod. "Why, yessir," she said to herself, doing her best to imitate a British accent. "Whatever you say, sir." In a matter of seconds, the heavy bulwark began creaking and squealing, as if protesting even this slow-motion activity. "Looks like you don't get much exercise," she told it as she drove through.

Around the next bend in the drive, Hope finally caught sight of the house. No stone lions stood guard on either side of the front door, but the house didn't need any to be impressive. With mouth agape and eyes wide, she stared through the windshield. The front face of the house—three stories tall and at least as wide—was more glass than weathered wood. Low, sculpted shrubs hugged the façade.

As soon as Hope stepped from her car, a tail-wagging black lab greeted her, zig-zagging along the red brick sidewalk ahead of her and stopping now and then to make sure Hope hadn't lost her way. The dog led her over a wooden bridge and through a Japanese garden, complete with bonsai, stone benches, colorful lanterns, and a gently bubbling fountain.

This is Ethan Burke's house? she marveled, touching a fingertip to a small, shiny leaf on the ball-shaped boxwood beside the front steps. Never in a million years would she have pictured him in a—

The door swung open so quickly that Hope lurched with surprise.

"Sorry," Ethan said, smiling sheepishly, "didn't mean to scare you."

She giggled nervously. "Don't mind me," she said, accepting his one-armed invitation into the mansion. "I've been the jumpy type my whole life. Why, my folks used to say—"

Hope bit her lower lip. *Why are you chattering like a magpie? You're here to help that sweet little girl, not to pay this ladies' man a social visit....*

"Your folks used to say what?" he asked, closing the door.

What he doesn't know can't hurt you, she said to herself. She shrugged. "That I was jumpy...."

Ethan chuckled and grinned, and it took her off guard. Another item to add to her quickly growing "Why Women Love Ethan" list. But really, smile or no smile, he looked even more handsome now than when he'd come to her office in a dark business suit. Its cut and color had made it impossible *not* to notice his barrel chest and his narrow waist and hips. And the starched white collar of his shirt had only served to make his slightly tanned face all the more obvious. There was no denying he was a handsome man. His suit, his stance, his *style* made him look smart and sexy and successful all at the same time. But now, in maroon leather loafers, softly faded khakis, and a cream-colored silk shirt, he looked relaxed, casual, down-to-earth.

"Never mix business with pleasure" had always been Hope's professional motto, and she'd never broken the self-imposed rule. Had never been tempted to. Until now.

It was more than the clothes and the smile. Hope had pegged Ethan as an English hunt-club type. A guy who liked big, clunky wood furnishings and dark plaid upholstery. *Wrong again!* she thought, scanning the enormous foyer.

Skylights lit the room, making the pendant lamps of chrome and opaque glass unnecessary, even at this hour. With the lamps lit, a warm, golden glow shimmered down like muted sunshine, illuminating the large faux leopard skin tacked to one wall. On another wall, black-and-white photos of animals in the wild captured her attention. "Those are beautiful," she ventured, openly admiring the pictures of zebras, lions, and giraffes. "Where did you buy them?"

"Didn't."

She glanced over her shoulder at him. "Didn't what?"

"Didn't buy them," he said matter-of-factly. "I took them myself."

Hope faced the photo wall again. "*You* took those?"

He shrugged, as if aiming a camera at exotic creatures was no big deal at all. "I thought a safari might cure what ailed me a couple of winters back."

She gave the rest of the space a quick once-over. "And what could possibly ail a man like you?"

His left eyebrow rose as if to say, "A man like me?" Instead, he said, "Boredom, emptiness, lack of purpose...you name it."

Boredom? Hope was incredulous.

He gave another shrug. "When you've done it all...."

She couldn't help but wonder if he'd managed to leave the negative feelings behind on the African veld, or if he still coped with nagging pessimism—even while living in the lap of luxury.

Her hands clasped behind her back, Hope pretended to study the large, full-color shot of a lion pride sprawled paws-over-whiskers beneath a gnarled acacia tree. "Our lives are what we make them, Mr. Burke," she said quietly. "I think maybe it's up to us to create our own sense of purpose." She paused, then added, "So did it?"

He cleared his throat. "Cure what ailed me, you mean?"

Hope nodded.

Slowly, Ethan shook his head. "Not really."

She contemplated his words, remembering that out front, she'd parked her sensible sedan beside a racy, low-slung red convertible that was tethered to a shiny trailer carrying an iridescent blue hang glider. He owned acres of riverfront property, lived in a literal mansion, had the financial wherewithal to travel to faraway lands…surely, he wasn't serious about being *bored!*

Hope wondered what made him think he could raise an emotionally distraught orphan with an attitude like that. But then, guilt began to tug at the corners of her mind. *Give him a break,* she told herself. *At least he's willing to try.* Which was more than she could say for some folks.…

She smiled and faced him, preparing to ask where Molly was and when they might begin their session. If she'd known how it would affect her—seeing the way he looked against the backdrop of life-sized wooden giraffes, zebra paintings, and towering plants—Hope wouldn't have turned around. It seemed to her that Ethan Burke *belonged* in that setting with his rugged good looks and Jack Hanna getup.

She recalled bits and pieces of the information gleaned from her online research: he'd raced stock cars. Had flown twin-engine planes. Climbed mountains. Sailed the seven seas. Yet he'd come right out and admitted that his thrilling life hadn't thrilled *him.* Now her heart ached for little Molly, and she wondered how Ethan would feel about a child who, with her grief and misery, would tether him to one spot indefinitely. If everything he'd experienced in life had left him feeling empty, what did he have, really, to offer a needy little girl?

Would Molly be made to feel like a ball and chain, the way Hope had felt as a child? Or, worse, would she be just one more possession to show off at summer soirees before being trotted off to some fancy, faraway boarding school?

Well, Hope thought grimly, *at least she'd be at the best boarding school money could buy.*

Ethan chuckled softly. "You look as though you've just stepped into the Twilight Zone." He punctuated his observation by whistling a few notes from the show's theme song.

Hope didn't know what to say, so she let a quiet giggle suffice as a reply. Just then, Ethan's big black lab rescued her by trotting up and sitting at her feet, his chocolate-brown eyes pleading for attention. An animal lover for as long as she could remember, Hope got down on her knees and took the dog's face in her hands. "So, what's it like living at the zoo, big fella?"

A quiet, breathy bark was his answer.

As she got to her feet, she asked Ethan, "What's his name?"

"Dino."

She looked at the dog and gave his head an affectionate pat. "Funny, he doesn't look Italian."

Ethan laughed. "I didn't name him. The neighbors did."

In response to her inquiring expression, he added, "He's here often enough to be mine, though." Pocketing his hands, he said, "All the perks of a pet without the vet bills. But best of all, Molly loves him."

"I'm sure he's good for her. Especially now."

"Molly's quite a kid. But I imagine you already learned that."

At the mention of the child's name, the dog's ears perked up.

"She's in her room, fella," Ethan said, bending to scratch Dino's chin. "Go on, and tell her she has company; you'll save me a trip upstairs...."

Dino bounded up the curved wooden staircase and disappeared through a doorway at the top. "Hurry, boy!" Hope called after him, feigning alarm. "Timmy's trapped in the well, and we've gotta get help!" Giggling, she added, "If he actually brings her down here, I'll eat my hat."

"You're not wearing a hat."

She matched his smile, tooth for tooth. "Then I'll get one."

No sooner had she spoken than Dino appeared on the landing. He barked once, then sat on his haunches and looked over his shoulder, waiting for Molly to join him.

Ethan put his back to the staircase and whispered, "The only time there seems to be a spark of life in her eyes is when she's with that dog."

Hope couldn't help but notice the way Ethan's smile brightened at the sight of Molly. He took a step forward, gripped the railing, and looked up at her, as if giving in to some unconscious, magnetic pull. He loved her like his own daughter, and it was written all over his face.

A magical moment ticked by before Hope broke the silence. "Well, there she is, Mr. Burke. Good for what ails you."

❧

When counselor and patient emerged from Ethan's teak-paneled den at the conclusion of the therapy session, Hope's senses were overwhelmed by the steamy scents reminiscent of a five-star Italian restaurant. "I don't know about you," she said, giving Molly's hand an affectionate squeeze, "but now I'm *glad* I said I'd stay for supper!"

Her first inclination had been to politely turn down the invitation. Ethan must have read the latent response in her expression, because he'd quickly added, "I'm sure it will be good for Molly...."

Now, Hope glanced at the girl, whose only response had been the quirk of one dark eyebrow. On the chance that the minuscule change in Molly's expression had meant that she *wanted* Hope to stay, she'd said yes.

But she'd expected boiled hot dogs and pork 'n beans. Or grilled cheese sandwiches and canned tomato soup. Pizza, even, or subs, delivered by a teenage boy in a baseball cap.

"I hope you like stuffed shells," Ethan said as they entered the kitchen.

"If they taste even half as good as they smell, I think I'll like them just fine!"

For a second, she would have sworn Molly had mirrored his smile. But the girl quickly averted her gaze and focused on the black-and-white tile floor beneath her pink-sneakered feet. She looked so small, so vulnerable, that Hope gave in to the sudden urge to hug her. Getting on her knees, she placed her hands on Molly's slender shoulders. "You've taste-tested your uncle Ethan's stuffed shells before, haven't you?"

The instant of eye contact was deep and intense, and Hope knew better than to waste the precious moment. "You should've warned me," she added with a grin and a wink, "and I wouldn't have eaten those cookies he brought in earlier." She punctuated the joke with a light kiss on the tip of Molly's nose, then stood and draped an arm around her...and it warmed her to the soles of her feet when the child didn't fight it.

Ethan plopped a hot baking dish onto a wicker trivet, then removed his thick oven mitts. "You don't mind eating in the kitchen, do you?"

"Actually, I prefer it," Hope admitted. "The kitchen is my favorite room in any house."

Smiling, he nodded. "Make yourself comfortable while I pour the iced tea."

"What can I do to help?"

"Not a thing," he said, watching as Molly slid onto the caned seat of a ladder-back chair. The way she sat—eyes downcast and hands primly folded on the tile-topped table—made Hope wonder if she might be praying. *But what are you praying for, little one? Your mommy and daddy to come back?*

Hope understood that desire only too well. If she had a dollar for every time she'd said that same prayer....

She took a deep breath and sat down across from Molly, reminding herself that if she hoped to keep her professional distance, she'd have to watch herself closely. This kid reminded her entirely too much of her own childhood.

A cursory assessment would suggest that the sweet-faced girl had nothing at all in common with Hope. For starters, Molly had gleaming black hair, while Hope's freckled face was framed by a wild mane of fiery curls. Molly saw the world through dark, almond-shaped eyes; Hope's were long-lashed and green.

There, the most salient differences ended.

Both were tiny and feminine, and they moved in fits and starts like small birds skittering among fallen leaves in search of nourishment, companionship, *family*.

Both had been traumatized by the loss of their parents early in life.

Both were alone in the world.

But that wasn't entirely true. Molly had Ethan....

"Shall we say grace?" he asked, taking his place at the head of the table.

Hope blinked in surprise, which inspired a quiet laugh from Ethan. "I haven't been a regular churchgoer," he stated, flapping a white linen napkin across his knees, "but that's going to change." He glanced at Molly, who sat silent and still, staring into her empty plate. "She needs the community and support of a parish family. Never more than now."

Nodding, Hope said, "I couldn't agree more."

"And when I have to be out of town on business, I know just the family that'll give it to her."

If he doled out much more warmth, Hope thought, she might roast from the inside out!

He folded his hands and shot her an amused grin. "Let me guess...you're wondering what a guy like me sounds like when he talks to God...."

She blushed slightly and stared down at her own plate. How did he know precisely what she was thinking?

Without further comment, he closed his eyes and bowed his head. "Father, we thank You for this food and for blessing us with good health and the protection of a safe home."

When he paused, Hope found herself criticizing his words, because how would a footloose and fancy-free guy like him know the difference between a good home and a lousy one?

"Thank You, too," Ethan continued, "for sending Miss Majors into our lives. Bless her with Your loving wisdom so she'll know how to help my sweet Molly find her voice again." He reached across the table and laid one hand atop the child's. "'Cause I sure do miss hearing her say how much she loves me...." His smooth, resonant voice cracked slightly, and he cleared his throat. "Amen" came on the heels of a gruff, growly breath.

"Amen," Hope echoed.

Ethan grabbed a long-handled spoon and scooped up two shells, depositing both on Molly's plate. "Extra sauce on top?" he asked. And without waiting for a reply, he traded spoon for ladle and poured thick, spicy sauce over her meat-and-spinach-filled pasta. "Of course you do," he said, grinning nervously. "You love Italian food smothered in sauce, don't you?"

"I'd like to meet the person who *doesn't* love it!" Hope said.

"My father, for starters...."

Hope helped herself to a dipper of extra sauce while Ethan sprinkled grated parmesan over Molly's meal, then his own. "Why?" she asked. "He doesn't like garlic? Oregano?"

"No...Dad's just...different."

Was it her imagination, or did Ethan seem to harbor some sort of grudge against his father? Hope didn't dwell on the question long, because soon, she'd have the answer to that question—and more. And by the time she got Molly talking again, she'd know more about Ethan than he could ever have dreamed possible.

But she hadn't been right about him in any respect so far. What made her think he'd willingly open up and share personal, private information about his most intimate relationships?

"How's your iced tea, kiddo...sweet enough?" he asked Molly.

But the girl barely acknowledged him, poking sullenly at her food with one tine of her fork. The only sound she'd made since sitting down was the squeal of chair legs as she'd scooted closer to the table. Hope had noticed how she'd winced at the noise, as if it had disrupted the balance in her quiet, solitary world. She made a mental note to use musical instruments, television shows, CDs—a variety of sounds—at their next session to determine which of them elicited the strongest—and most positive—response.

Like a nervous mother hen, Ethan hovered. Sprinkling a little more cheese atop her sauce, he said, "Remember that time I found you sitting by the fridge with a spoon in one hand and your cheeks stuffed like a chipmunk's with Romano?" Laughing, he watched for a reaction.

Hope's heart ached for him, because despite his female magnetism, which came without much effort, he seemed to be putting his "all" into interacting with this girl—but to no avail. Most people in his situation would try for a few weeks, at best, before throwing in the towel. To his credit, he'd stuck it out for months

now, and Hope knew with certainty he'd stick it out for the dura-
tion. She gave him credit for that.

Hope glanced furtively at Ethan. Was he aware that when
he looked at Molly, his love for her was as evident as the dab of
tomato sauce on his chin? Yes, he was trying, all right. Smiling,
Hope tacked a line onto the prayer he'd said at the start of the
meal: *Lord, help me reach her...for Ethan's sake, as well as her own.*

Chapter Three

E than eased the covers under Molly's chin. "You comfy, sweetie? Got enough pillows? Is the blanket too heavy?"

He heaved a sad sigh. *Might as well be talking to myself.* But he shouldn't have been disappointed; she hadn't responded in any way since that awful moment in Sam and Shari's London flat when she'd finally accepted the fact that her mom and dad were gone for good.

That was three long months ago!

He'd dedicated himself these past weeks to her one-on-one care. Except for the three to four hours every day when he absolutely had to be at the office—when Maria watched over her—he'd spent every moment with this precious child. He'd obtained permission to keep her out of school, at least until there'd been some progress with the counseling.

On his knees now, Ethan sandwiched her hands between his own. "Lord Jesus," he prayed aloud, "send Your strongest, smartest angels to watch over my sweet Molly tonight. Bless her with beautiful dreams, and let the sunshine kiss her awake in the morning. And remind her how very much her uncle Ethan loves her. Amen."

He tried to remember if she'd been three or four when he'd made up that prayer just for her. She'd loved it and had memorized it almost from the very first recitation. During Ethan's visits to London and the Sylvesters' trips to his place, she'd always say it with him, her lilting soprano harmonizing with his deep baritone.

Ethan had repeated the prayer every night since Molly had come to live with him, but the words always sounded hollow and flat without the music of her voice. So was it habit that made him persist in praying it? Or was it pure stubbornness?

Stubbornness, he decided as he got to his feet, *because I intend to say it every night for the rest of her life!* Bending down low, he pressed a paternal kiss to her forehead. "G'night, Molly, m'love," he whispered, and when she closed her black-lashed eyes, he kissed her again and then waited...hoping....

Each time Ethan had stayed with Sam and Shari in London, Molly had insisted that her uncle Ethan tuck her in every night of his visit. The ritual had started when Molly was still in diapers: Shari would feign impatience as she instructed the child to go to bed; Molly, dressed in a ruffly nightgown, would dawdle until Ethan lumbered up the steps behind her, pretending that the last thing he wanted to do was tuck her into bed.

She'd known as well as her parents how much Ethan treasured their little game, and, as if to prove it, she'd wrap her arms around his neck and squeeze for all she was worth. "I *love* you, Uncle Ethan!" would echo from every wall of her pretty pink bedroom as she snuggled into her blankets, wiggling her eyebrows with a mischievous glint sparkling in her dark eyes. "Will you read me a story?" she'd ask, a fingertip between her lips.

He'd "reluctantly" agree...and read book after book until she fell asleep.

They'd played the game last Christmas. Could it really have been just nine months ago? She'd been so happy and well-adjusted, secure in the belief that Mom and Dad and Uncle Ethan would always be there for her.

Would she ever feel that safe, that sheltered, again?

Ethan's fists clenched at his sides. *Yes, she will*, he vowed, *even if I have to move heaven and earth to make it happen!*

She looked so sweet, so innocent, lying in the middle of the queen-sized bed. He wanted nothing more than to shield her from all pain. But he couldn't do that, especially since she refused to tell him what was wrong.

He settled for a hug. "Ahh, sweetie," he said, gathering her close, stroking her silken black hair, "I sure do miss you. Miss you *so much*!"

Her only response was a long, shuddering breath.

Gently, Ethan tucked the covers back around her and plumped her pillows. "Won't you tell me what's wrong, darlin'?"

Silence.

Sitting on the edge of her bed, he lifted her chin on a bent forefinger until their gazes locked. "I'd do anything, *anything* for you. You know that, don't you?"

He'd said it before, hundreds of times in the months since Sam and Shari's accident, yet Ethan hoped that tonight, maybe, she'd say, "Yes, I know...."

Molly stared deep into his eyes, and for the first time since he'd brought her into his home, Ethan believed she was really *seeing* him. There was a certain light, a new intensity in the dark, shining orbs that he hadn't seen since....

...Since before he'd told her Sam and Shari were dead.

"Whatever you want, honey, you name it and it's yours. I promise."

Her brows drew together, as if to say, "Promise? Ha!" But even that slight response heightened his hope. "I've never broken a promise to you, have I?"

The little furrow in her brow deepened. He read it as a no, taking heart in the belief that she at least trusted him. The fingers of his right hand formed the Boy Scout salute. "I give you my word, Molly. Tell me what you want, and I'll get it for you."

She lay quietly, alternately blinking and staring, for what seemed like an hour. He watched with rapt attention as her chin quivered and she inhaled a shallow breath.

Was she...was she going to *talk*?

Ethan held his own breath and sat perfectly still. He couldn't, *wouldn't* risk a sound or movement that might cause her to change her mind. *Please, God,* he prayed silently, *please....*

Her eyes widened, and her lower lip trembled.

Lord Almighty in heaven, please....

Surely God had it in mind to answer Ethan's heartfelt prayers. Eventually. *Right, Lord?*

Molly's lips formed a thin, taut line as tears welled up in her eyes. She sighed audibly, gave a brief shake of her head, and then turned away, as if to say, "Don't make promises you can't keep."

Because, of course, she wanted only one thing. She wanted her mom and dad back, and he couldn't make that wish come true no matter how many strings he pulled, no matter how many dollars he spent. He understood, suddenly, that his repeated promises to give her anything sounded like the shallow, superficial oath of a desperate man.

But I am desperate!

He couldn't afford to wallow in self-pity, however. Molly would remain at the center of his focus. He'd be there for her the way he hadn't been for his mother, for Bess. He hadn't been man enough to save *them*, but by all that was holy, he'd do everything in his power to save this kid—or die trying.

On his feet again, Ethan brushed back Molly's bangs, hoping she wouldn't notice his trembling fingers. "Silly of me to make promises I can't keep," he said. "I should've known you're way too smart to fall for a line like that."

He swallowed and said a quick, silent prayer that God would give him the strength and the inspiration to say something, anything, that would comfort her—right this minute—because she needed comfort *now*.

"I can promise you this," he said, his voice rasping on a pent-up sob, "I love you, Molly-girl. I've loved you from the moment I first set eyes on you, and I'll love you all the days of my life."

For the second time in as many minutes, she looked at him. *Really* looked at him. He'd told her before that he loved her, probably thousands of times over the years. And except for those months before she'd learned to talk, she'd always echoed the words. Would she say them now? Was it too much to hope?

Lord, he prayed again, *please....*

As suddenly as she'd let him into her solitary, silent little world, she squeezed her eyes shut, turned toward the wall, and shut him out again. If God planned to answer Ethan's prayer, it obviously wouldn't be tonight. *She's in Your hands now, Lord*, he thought, pulling her bedroom door closed behind him. And as he shuffled down the hall, he wondered how many times he'd say *that* before this was over.

The soles of his sneakers squeaked as he made his way down the polished hardwood steps and headed across the foyer. He stopped for a minute, hands in his pockets, and stood staring at the intricate pattern beneath his feet.

In keeping with the jungle theme in this room, he'd sent to Malaysia for the wood. And it had taken nearly six months to interview a dozen craftsmen in search of the one who could turn Ethan's rough sketches into reality. It had been well worth the wait, because the man he'd hired was a true artist. The honeyed teak was inlaid with a lion and a lamb, carved from mahogany, lying side by side beneath a small tree. The scene was amazingly lifelike, from the light reflected in the animals' gentle gazes to the veins in each leaf above them.

Evidence of Ethan's ability to "pull strings" and "make things happen" didn't end there. Most of the carpets had been imported from Persia; hammered brass urns from Morocco and hand-blown glass vases from Italy decorated tables he'd purchased in Brazil.

When he'd made it known that he had his eye on a writing table that had once belonged to a czar, everyone had said he'd never talk the Russian government into letting him buy it, but he did. And no one had believed he'd ever convince the family of a silent-film star to part with the one-of-a-kind four-poster bed in which Molly was now sleeping.

"Put enough digits ahead of the decimal," he'd assured the doubters, "and *nothing* is priceless."

He ran a hand over the smooth top of the writing table that now stood near his front door. Yes, he'd gotten pretty good at pulling strings to get what he wanted, but his formerly prized acquisitions gave him no comfort, brought him no pleasure. And this time, being "connected" wouldn't do him a whit of good. This time, money couldn't buy what he was lacking.

What did the well-traveled businessman who lived in a riverfront mansion, who owned a garage filled with antique roadsters and pricey sports cars, lack?

His best friends, Sam and Shari, for starters.

And the soul-satisfying sound of Molly's voice.

He caught a quick mental glimpse of her, looking for all the world like a fragile porcelain doll against the starched white sheets.

Shaking his head, he again tried to figure out *why* Molly's silence made him feel completely helpless.

But he knew the answer. It was his fault she'd stopped talking. He'd blundered into her flat like a bull in a china shop and had blurted out the truth like a clumsy oaf, shocking her so badly that it was possible she would never recover.

The admission made his heart pound.

Ethan ran a hand through his hair and headed for the kitchen, his footsteps echoing in the big, bright room. The refrigerator motor hummed. Ice *kerchunked* into the plastic bin in the freezer. The dishwasher droned. Fluorescent overhead lights buzzed. The cabinet door squeaked when he opened it to get a glass, and the crescent-shaped ice cubes clinked and cracked as he filled it with gurgling water. The Westminster chimes of the carriage clock in the kitchen hutch announced it was 8:45.

He'd never been aware of all this *noise* before. Why was he noticing it now?

He knew the answer to that, too. Usually, the house was brimming with guests.

If he'd invited government officials, visiting foreign dignitaries, entertainers, and authors because he'd enjoyed their companionship, it would have been one thing. But the fact of the matter was, he usually kept the house bustling with activity because he couldn't stand the silence. He couldn't stand being alone.

And who could blame him? If any of those VIPs knew what sort of man he truly was, they wouldn't want to be alone with him, either.

He didn't like himself, and the reason was simple. As he saw it, he had a character flaw of immeasurable proportions; a deficiency, a defect that cut so deep, he couldn't even come up with a name for it. Whatever it was, well.... *Three strikes and you're out, Burke....*

For the second time that night, Ethan shook off a horrible memory. He was about to take a sip of water when it dawned on him. The cut-crystal goblet was part of a collection that had belonged to a Hawaiian king. It hadn't been easy finding the matching pitcher in a Civil War shop. If he sold either, he could easily pay cash for one of those subcompact cars the teenagers were driving these days.

He started chuckling. It was ridiculous, really—his sitting here in the lap of luxury. What was the point of having it all if "it all" was useless in helping the people he loved?

Soon, his rumbling laughter was echoing off every wall in the cavernous kitchen. Tears sprang to his eyes as he wheezed and chortled, one hand repeatedly slapping his thigh, the other clutching the footed drinking glass.

He didn't know when, exactly, his tears of mirth turned into tears of another kind. All Ethan knew was that he didn't *like* feeling helpless. Hadn't liked it when his father had deserted his mother years back; hadn't liked it when she'd grieved herself to death over it.

There was no noise. No conversation. No "good host" duties to help him escape his dark thoughts this time. He'd deliberately cleared the house of partygoers and long-term guests to ensure that Molly had a tranquil haven where she could adjust to her new life and accept that....

...That the guy who's in charge of her doesn't have a clue. About anything.

As usual, the helpless feelings reminded Ethan what an irresponsible lout he was.

Bess's accident had been his fault, after all. He'd believed it at fourteen, and he believed it now. If he'd gone to summer camp with her that year, as he'd done every year before, she'd never have fallen on the pier. He would have seen to it that she didn't go where she shouldn't.

But you didn't want her tagging along everywhere you went. You didn't want the guys razzing you about your four-foot-tall shadow.

It was his own immature selfishness that he blamed for the accident that had left his sister wheelchair-bound and nearly deaf. And his stubborn streak had been the reason for her death ten years later.

Emotionally spent, Ethan put the glass onto the table with a *thump*. He'd let an awful lot of people down....

That belief had fueled his main ambition in life: to make money—more than anyone could imagine possible—to pay for the harm he'd caused.

In the years since Bess's death, he'd been doggedly determined to see that her memory, at least, lived on. So, he'd donated money to dozens of charities, funded the additions of new wings to hospitals, paid to put the latest equipment into school computer labs and the great works of literature in their libraries...all in Bess's name.

But just as his money couldn't erase his guilt and shame, it also couldn't help Molly. He'd called in every favor. He'd spent hours on the Internet and even more hours on the phone searching for *the* top specialist, the great expert, the one miracle worker who could get his Molly talking again and put her back on the path of the living.

He slumped onto the seat of the very chair in which Miss Majors had sat earlier. Ironic that her name was Hope—because she was his last hope. The even greater irony was that if she could help Molly, it would cost him next to nothing!

The carriage clock he'd purchased at Asprey in London began counting out the nine o'clock hour, each hollow note reminding him how truly alone he was.

But wait.

He wasn't alone.

He had Molly!

And she has you.

Ethan rubbed his eyes and shook his head. *What a wicked joke life's played on the poor kid,* he thought, *making an orphan of her first as an infant and then again when Sam and Shari died, then sticking her with a guardian who is helpless and powerless to do anything for her that really matters.*

Something shiny winked up at him from the floor, and Ethan crouched down to pick it up. "Hmm," he said distractedly, inspecting it, "a butterfly earring..."

It belonged to Hope Majors. Had to. Because Molly didn't wear anything but ladybugs and daisies, and Maria's choice of earrings had always been gold hoops.

He dried his eyes on the cuff of his shirt and pictured Hope— wide, green eyes and curly, coppery hair. He didn't think he'd ever seen longer, thicker eyelashes or a sweeter, more sincere smile. Her voice was softly soothing, every word reminding him of wind chimes...and those tiny, silver bells his mom used to put on the Christmas tree. And despite the fact that she was barely bigger than a minute, Hope seemed to have more spunk and spark in her curvy little body than any woman he'd known.

If anyone can get through to Molly, she can, he thought, closing his fingers around the butterfly.

Then he opened his hand and put the earring in his other palm. Had her father given it to her? A brother? He didn't like the possibility that it might have been a gift from a boyfriend. Or, worse yet, a fiancé. *You only just met the woman, Burke, and she's Molly's counselor, for the love of Pete.*

But given a choice between the green-eyed monster and self-loathing, he'd take the beast any day.

A slow smile spread across his face as he took another sip of cool water. Nodding, Ethan dropped the earring into his shirt pocket. *First thing in the morning,* he thought, giving his pocket a pat, *I'll call her.* "Anything missing?" he'd ask. And she'd probably say, "Only one of my favorite earrings...." And that's when he'd invite her to lunch, a two-birds-with-one-stone meal, during which he could quiz her about Molly's progress and return her little silver butterfly.

The carriage clock ticked quietly now, counting off the seconds with mechanical precision. He knew that it had never been more than eight seconds slow. If it said 9:07, then it was seven minutes after nine, meaning he'd have to wait nearly twelve full hours to make a call to Hope's Rockville office.

He turned off the overhead lights and headed upstairs, thinking that maybe tonight he would read one of the books that had been cluttering his nightstand for months. Maria would sure be glad to have one less book to dust....

Or maybe he'd watch some television—if he could remember how to make the flat-screen TV appear from behind the wooden panels covering its wall mount.

Carrying his water goblet onto the balcony off of his room, Ethan sat in one of the showy deckchairs he'd ordered from that high-priced outfit in New York and watched the moonlight shimmering on the Potomac. He caught himself praying this feeling would never disappear.

He was a fool. He knew that better than anyone. But he couldn't put the pretty little therapist out of his mind. She'd been aptly named, he thought.

And then an idea formed in his head....

Maybe hope was the thing he'd been searching for, that elusive, missing puzzle piece that always made him feel incomplete.

And maybe Hope Majors would help him find it.

Chapter Four

M iss Majors, please."

"This is Hope...."

It wasn't quite nine o'clock, but it didn't surprise Ethan that she was already in her office. Nor did it surprise him that she'd answered her phone on the first ring. Ethan smiled, for he'd recognized her voice instantly. For one thing, he'd never heard another like it. For another, he'd been hearing it all through the night in his dreams.

Her small counseling practice was affiliated with Rockville General Hospital, and she probably didn't earn enough to hire a receptionist. "The reason I'm calling," he began, clearing his throat, "is that I found a butterfly earring under the kitchen table after you left. And since Molly hasn't pierced her ears yet, and Maria hasn't developed a fondness for this particular species, I figured it must be yours."

He could almost see her grabbing one earlobe and then the other to see which one was missing.

"So *that's* where it is!"

"Maybe if you have time for lunch, I can return it. I have a few questions to ask you about Molly's treatment."

He heard the unmistakable sound of Velcro and presumed she'd opened her daily planner.

"I'm free after one," she said, "if that isn't too late for lunch."

A quick glance at his own calendar showed a one o'clock meeting to discuss the expansion of one of his smaller holdings, a printing firm in Baltimore's enterprise zone. The senator was a busy woman, and it had taken two weeks of telephone tag to get this appointment. If he canceled now, there was no telling when he'd get another chance to speak with her. So Ethan couldn't believe his own ears when he said, "One is fine."

"Where would you like me to meet you?"

Right here, right now, he wanted to blurt out. "Ever been to Saxon's?" he heard himself say.

"No...where's that?"

He swallowed a note of disappointment. When he'd acquired the eatery a couple of years back, he'd launched a major advertising campaign, complete with television and radio ads. Obviously, they hadn't reached *all* of his intended audience. "It's on Rockville Pike," he said, "right before you—"

"Oh, you mean that place with the gigantic sword and shield on the sign?"

Amazing, he thought, *that tens of thousands of dollars didn't accomplish what a five-hundred-dollar sign did.* "That's the place!"

"I've heard they have a real French chef...."

She'd heard right. Ethan had flown to Paris to taste-test Henri's culinary concoctions before offering him the job. "So I hear...."

"Kinda weird, don't you think...? A French chef in a German-sounding restaurant?"

"Never gave it a thought," he admitted, remembering that Saxon's had a decent following when he bought it.

"...never been inside," she was saying, "so I hope I'm dressed appropriately." On the heels of a girlish giggle, Hope added, "Wouldn't want to embarrass you or anything."

Embarrass me? He pictured the sensible suit she'd been wearing the first time they'd met, followed by the slacks and light sweater she'd had on last night. *You could wear holey sneakers, raggedy blue jeans, and a bulky sweatshirt and still outshine most of the women in the place!* "I'm sure whatever you're wearing will be just fine."

From out of the blue, she asked, "Who's staying with Molly while you're at the office?"

It didn't surprise him that she asked. What surprised him was that it had taken this long for her to ask. "She's with Maria, my housekeeper." He hesitated. "The woman loves Molly almost as much as her own kids, and Molly feels the same way about her."

Hope must have heard his secretary's *buzz,* because she said, "Well, my nine-fifteen is here. See you at one!"

But because he didn't want to hang up, Ethan scrambled for something to say. "Right. One. I'll get there a few minutes early, try to snag us a booth near the windows so we'll have a river view."

"A river view?"

She sounded distracted, and he would've sworn he heard the sounds of an eraser, drumming on her desktop. *She's Molly's therapist, and you're carrying on like you just scheduled a romantic lunch!* As the heat of a blush warmed his cheeks, he said, "Right. One. See you then." And finally hung up.

He checked his Rolex and frowned. Quarter after nine. It wasn't like he didn't have plenty to occupy him between now and one o'clock. There was the meeting with the senator to reschedule, for starters. And his accountant would arrive any minute. Then, there was the matter of going over the household books with Maria....

But something told him it would still be a long four hours....

❦

Hope parked beside Ethan's racy sports car and took a deep breath as she checked her lipstick in the rearview mirror. Between appointments and all during the drive across town, she'd rehearsed what she intended to tell him as soon as their lunch was delivered.

First of all, she practiced in her head as she walked across the parking lot, *I'd like to suggest that you warm up the atmosphere of that house a bit, even if only in Molly's room.* That wasn't to say it wasn't an interesting place with all the eclectic collectibles scattered about. But the sleek angles of wood and glass, combined with the wild animal décor, made it feel more like a museum than a home. And maybe he could plan a shopping trip to buy girlie clothes, some stuffed animals, and feminine toys to help her adjust more quickly.

During the tour he'd given her of the mansion, those ideas had been on the tip of her tongue, and it had taken all her willpower *not* to recommend that he turn one of the guest rooms into a playroom. Though it had been nighttime when she'd seen the house, Hope could tell that during the day, sunshine would stream in through the tall arched windows. And with that view of the river....

She spotted Ethan the instant she stepped into the dining room. He'd chosen a table near the windows, just as he'd said he would. Backlit by the blue, cloud-dotted sky and wearing a brown pinstriped suit, he looked like a male cover model.

"May I help you, miss?" the maître d' asked, giving her a quick once-over.

"I'm here to meet that gentleman," she answered, pointing at Ethan.

The man tucked in his chin as if to say, "I'll take you over there, but if you ask me, you're way outta your league, missy." He shot her a stiff, well-practiced smile and said, "Of course, my dear." Tucking a gold-trimmed black leather menu under his tuxedoed arm, he added, "Follow me, please."

As they made their way across the plush carpet, Hope noted the deep-green custom drapery treatments topping every window, the rich upholstery on every mahogany chair, the brocade linens atop each table. Silver flatware clinked against china dinner plates as other patrons ate their meals, and the crystals of a dozen chandeliers rained rainbow light upon the goblets at each place setting.

"Miss Majors," Ethan said, standing up when she arrived at his table. "So good to see you again." He pulled out her chair and then returned to his own while the maître d' flapped a heavy linen napkin across her knees.

"Have you been waiting long?" she asked, taking the menu offered by the maître d'.

Ethan shook his head. "No, no; not long at all." He nodded at the man. "Jasper," he said, "bring the lady one of our special menus, will you please?"

The man took back her menu and bowed. "Yes, yes of course, Mr. Burke. Will there be anything else, sir?"

"That'll do for now," Ethan said, smiling.

Hope watched Jasper hurry away and whisper something to a tuxedoed fellow at the bar. The two chanced a peek toward Ethan's table, then disappeared around the corner. A second later, when a server in a starched black uniform poked her head out from behind the gilded partition, Hope met Ethan's gaze. "You must come here quite often."

He shrugged one shoulder. "Not really."

"But…everyone seems to know you."

Grinning, he gave a nonchalant wave of his hand. "Only 'cause I could have 'em fired."

Fired? That could mean only one of two things: either he knew the boss or he *was* the boss. Something told Hope it was the latter, and for a reason she couldn't explain, it made her nervous. She took a sip of ice water from the goblet and tried to think of a sensible response. When she'd read those articles about him on the Internet, she had joked to herself that he must have more money than Donald Trump. But from the looks of things, it hadn't been a joke, after all.

Jasper returned and handed Hope a menu bound in white leather.

"Thank you," she said.

"My great pleasure, miss," he replied, then disappeared.

While she pretended to peruse the restaurant's offerings, Ethan fumbled in his coat pocket and withdrew a white envelope.

"Hope—may I call you Hope?"

"I thought we got that settled last night: Hope and Ethan, for Molly's sake...."

"You're right, of course." He shrugged again. "Just want to make sure I'm not overstepping my bounds." Then, "Before I forget, I have something here for you."

He slid the envelope across the table, and when she reached for it, their fingers touched. The contact was quick, slight, and barely noticeable, but the effect was electric. A shiver ran down her neck, and she felt her face begin to redden. Fortunately, Ethan didn't seem to have noticed. "Ahh," she said, peeking inside the envelope, "the missing earring." Tucking it into her purse, she grinned. "These are number seventy-eight in my butterfly collection."

"Butterfly collection?"

She nodded. "Pressed wings, stained-glass ornaments, tap-estries—" Hope stopped abruptly when she noted how intently Ethan was looking at her. With a self-conscious toss of her head, she said, "You'll learn in time that it isn't wise to get me started talking about butterflies, because I could go on and on for hours!" Then, sitting up straighter, she folded her hands on the table. "But you wanted to talk about Molly...?"

"That can wait until lunch arrives."

Unnerved by his scrutiny, she sought refuge behind her menu. "Since you seem so familiar with the place," Hope said, peeking over it, "maybe you could recommend something? Otherwise, I'll just ask for my old standby."

"Which would be...?"

"Cheeseburger and fries."

Ethan leaned back and, smiling, looked out at the river. "I usually order the filet mignon," he said, meeting her eyes again. "Henri hand-selects the cuts, and I promise, you've never had a more tender steak."

When the server came back, Ethan spoke up for her. "The lady will have the filet—how do you like yours, Hope? Rare? Medium?"

She'd never had filet mignon for lunch in her life, but rather than admit it, she said, "Medium rare will be just fine."

"I'll have the same," he said. "And tell Henri to do his usual magic." Turning to Hope, he asked, "Would you like a glass of wine?"

"No, thanks. Never touch the stuff." She hesitated. "But don't let that stop you from—"

"Two fluted glasses of tonic water over cracked ice," he instructed the server.

"With a twist?" she put in.

Without missing a beat, he wrinkled his nose. "Nah. Don't feel like dancing."

"Thank you, sir," said the server.

And when she was gone, Hope smiled. *For a man about town, he sure has a corny sense of humor.* Admittedly, though, she found everything about him charming.

"You want to hear a good one? I actually own a vineyard here in Maryland, though I don't drink at all."

"Never?"

He shook his head. "Guess it doesn't fit the stereotype of guys like me, does it? Single, moneybags, teetotaler...."

She couldn't help but laugh. "I'm beginning to see that very little about you fits the stereotype, Mr. Burke."

"Ethan," he corrected her. "I thought we got all that settled last night."

"Touché!"

Suddenly, his expression grew serious, and he rubbed his chin as though he had something important to say but didn't know where to begin. On the heels of a deep breath, he leaned closer. "Do you mind if I ask you a favor, Hope?"

The way he looked at her with those soulful brown eyes of his made it hard for her to concentrate. "Of course not."

"Well, I've been thinking...." He stroked the broad chin again. "That house of mine is awfully...." He shook his head. "Well, let's just say it isn't the most child-friendly place." Reaching across the table, he blanketed one of her hands with his. "Do you suppose you could help me make it...." Now he frowned as if searching for just the right words. "...help me make it warmer, more welcoming, for Molly?"

Hope blinked. So, now she could add "mind reader" to the quickly growing list of his finer qualities. "Sure I will," she said, deftly slipping her hand from beneath his.

"And while you're at it, could you help me fill that big closet in her room? I mean, I know what sort of games she likes, but clothes?" He shrugged helplessly. "I don't have a clue."

Suddenly, a faraway look dulled his bright eyes, and his smile dimmed slightly. "I'll give you my credit card. Money is no object. And, of course, I'll pay you for your time, so that—"

"Ethan," she interrupted him, "I'm more than happy to help in any way I can, free of charge. It'll be fun filling her closet with cute outfits. But...."

"But what?"

"But you're going shopping with us. You're her father now, and it's important that you become an active participant in the things that affect her."

He stared off into space. "Okay, I'll clear some time on my calendar...."

Here we go, Hope thought, smirking inwardly, *the laundry list of excuses why he can't—*

His eyes met hers. "Is tomorrow too soon to start?"

"Tomorrow?!" Hope laughed. Once again, she'd underestimated him. "Tomorrow is Friday. I think we can wait until the weekend."

"Well, you're the expert. Whatever you think is best."

The arrival of their food interrupted the conversation, but once the steaks had been served and their glasses had been refilled, Ethan pulled out an electronic organizer and typed in "Hope and Molly, shopping" on Saturday.

"What time's good for you?" he asked, his slender finger poised above the tiny keyboard.

"Nine?"

And as he added it to the gadget, she hoped this wasn't just one of those "cooperate for a little while" things parents too often did....

⊚⊚

After lunch, Hope realized she would be late for her first afternoon appointment. Ethan remained seated at the table as she rushed off, using the excuse that he needed to check on a few things in the restaurant kitchen before heading back to the office. But the real reason he'd lagged behind was so that he could watch Hope without her *knowing* he was watching.

He could see the parking lot from his seat, and he observed her through the window as she crossed the lot in half the time it would have taken most women, her high-heeled shoes hitting the pavement with the surety and grace of a model on a runway. She had curves in places where other women didn't even *have* places, and he doubted a more animated face existed, even in cartoons.

She was vivacious and vital, more alive than anyone he'd ever known. From what he'd seen, Hope didn't do anything halfway. And if her reputation as a children's counselor wasn't proof enough of that, he had only to remember the way she'd oohed at the delicate texture of her steak and aahed at the creamy richness of the hot fudge sundae he'd insisted on ordering as dessert.

The tastefully elegant outfit Hope had worn told him she knew the difference between quality and quantity—and that she valued quality. It might be true that she didn't earn as much as many others in her profession, but it was clear that she knew how to spend her dollars wisely, as evidenced by the trim, tailored dress that accentuated her petite figure. But Ethan didn't know which he'd say he admired more—the way she wore her clothes or the fact that she knew how to shop for them.

He'd been so thrilled when she'd suggested that he join her and Molly on Saturday that he'd almost bellowed "All right!" in the middle of Saxon's elegant dining room. Instead, he'd nodded somberly and said, "Good, that sounds good."

He watched Hope climb into her car and check the mirrors before backing out of her parking space with the deftness of a professional truck driver. He had to reel himself in as she drove off; he'd been leaning into the window as if doing so might allow him to ride along with her, if only for a moment.

Once she was out of sight, he sat back and exhaled the breath he hadn't even realized he'd been holding. And then his trusty Rolex beeped 2:15.

A quick mental calculation told him it would be a day and a half—nearly forty-eight hours!—until he'd see her again. He sneered at the watch and muttered, "For six thousand bucks, you'd think you could make time go a little faster."

"Excuse me, Mr. Burke?"

The heat of embarrassment pulsed in Ethan's cheeks as he looked into the questioning face of his maître d'. "Nothing, Jasper," he said, standing up. As he headed for the exit, he grinned to himself and muttered, "…except I think maybe I'm losin' it!"

Chapter Five

At Hope's suggestion, Ethan called the pastor's wife on Friday to inquire about the children's Sunday school program at church. It was important, she'd said, to keep Molly engaged in normal, everyday life. Exposure to other kids— their activities and bright voices—might inspire her to open up.

Ethan wasn't surprised when Mrs. Cummings began talking about Hope. The elderly woman's reputation as a matchmaker went way, way back, and it gave him the perfect excuse to find out more about the pretty counselor.

Hope was working closely with his beloved godchild, after all, so it made sense for him to want to know everything possible about her as a professional. But, sadly, Ethan hadn't managed to learn much of anything about her on a personal level.

Over their dinner of stuffed shells two nights prior, he'd asked her a few seemingly innocuous questions about herself, but she'd dodged them like a woman who'd rather walk a mile barefoot in the snow than divulge even the smallest tidbit about herself. "Where were you born?" and "Where does your family live?" were sidestepped as artfully as if he'd asked for her ATM PIN.

"Such a lovely girl," Mrs. Cummings was saying. "She deserves a lot of credit, turning out the way she did, considering...."

When the woman's voice trailed off, the hairs on the back of Ethan's neck bristled. "Considering what?"

The pastor's wife lowered her voice. "You were probably too young to remember, but the story was in all the papers the year Hope was born. It was quite the scandal!"

If that was true, he could look it up online later. But something told Ethan that Mrs. Cummings might just be able to add something that wouldn't have appeared in the newspaper articles. "A scandal?" he echoed.

"Oh, yes…it was terrible, I tell you. Simply terrible! When her father found out that her mother was with child, he ran off and left her."

Ethan blew a stream of air through his teeth, thinking it was downright sinful the way some husbands felt no responsibility toward their wives and children. The fact that desertion happened as often as it did sickened him. If *he'd* been blessed with a loving spouse and kids, there was no way he'd leave them!

"It really bothers me," he admitted, "when husbands don't honor their commitments."

Mrs. Cummings's sigh rattled in his ears. "Her father was never married to her mother, poor dear. In fact," she whispered, "he denied even the *possibility* that Abbie's baby might be his."

Abbie, he repeated mentally. Hope was a real person now, with an identity, as well as a life story. "Was she…was Abbie… promiscuous?"

"I should say not! She was young, and like most people her age, thought she knew everything. It was foolish, getting involved with that *Josephs* fellow."

Wincing, Ethan shook his head. "Fathers abandon young mothers on a daily basis. Why would a story like that be of any interest to the media?"

The pastor's wife gasped with exasperation. "Honestly! Sometimes I wonder why the good Lord made men so *dense!*" She paused and then lowered her voice again as she said, "Now, mind you, I'm telling you all of this only because Hope is working so closely with your little goddaughter." She hesitated before continuing, then said, "And it isn't as if I'm telling you anything you couldn't easily find out on your own...."

She was doing a lot of talking, he thought, but so far, the woman hadn't said much of anything. "You have my word," Ethan told her, "that anything you share with me is in the vault, and you're the only one with the combination."

"If you promise...," she said.

Just get on with it, please! he demanded silently.

And as if she'd read his thoughts, Mrs. Cummings cleared her throat. "Hope's mother had a twin named Alice. The poor girls lost their parents when they were barely seventeen. Alice, the quiet one, seemed to go into a shell after the accident, while Abbie seemed determined to see how far she could push the limits of ladylike decorum. She was eighteen when she met Taylor. That leather jacket and noisy motorcycle were almost as attractive as his big, green eyes and thick, coppery curls. And it didn't hurt, I suppose, that he was a TV star...."

Taylor Josephs. *Now* Ethan knew why the name sounded so familiar. Hope's father had been the host of a major network talk show based in Baltimore.

"Well, the dear girl came to us one Sunday morning after services, sobbing hysterically because she was in a family way. At first, she wouldn't reveal who the father was. But once the truth was out, and everybody in town knew the lowlife had denied being the baby's father, she spent the remainder of her pregnancy—nearly six months—alone in her room."

Mrs. Cummings continued with a catch in her voice. "She got a job as a bank teller, don't you know, and one Saturday after work, while Alice was working at the diner, Abbie put little Hope in her crib with her favorite teddy and a bottle of milk...."

The woman paused, and Ethan could hear her sniffling. He wondered what, exactly, Hope's mother had done. Run off like Taylor, maybe?

"She went into the bathroom and hanged herself," Mrs. Cummings finally managed. "She left a two-page suicide note explaining herself. Alice found it, and she showed it to Pastor Cummings after the funeral. When I read it, I bawled like a baby, I tell you!"

Sniffing, she continued. "About a year after Abbie's death, I suppose it was, Alice married John Majors, the bank vice president, and they raised little Hope as their own. By the time she was old enough for school, John had legally adopted her. They were good people, Alice and John, but I don't think either of them ever got over what happened to Abbie. And intentionally or not, they took their frustrations out on little Hope. Not that they were physically abusive or anything, but they were awfully strict. And cold. You'd never have guessed a child lived in that house. Not a toy in sight, not even a doll baby.

"They were devout people," she added in a raspy whisper, "but their faith was expressed in an angry, bitter, self-righteous way." A sigh, and then, "I never have been able to understand how anyone could know the Lord—truly know Him—and not feel...*happy!*" Another sigh. "They meant well, I suppose, but Hope didn't have much of a childhood, I'm afraid."

"Are they still alive?"

"No. Boating accident, about five years ago...."

Ethan sat in stunned silence, trying to sort out his thoughts. No wonder Hope had taken such an immediate interest in Molly!

And just when he thought Mrs. Cummings had finished her story, she said, "When Hope was about fifteen, she heard something in the attic and went up there to investigate. Found some evidence of mice…and a dusty old box tucked under the eaves. Inside was her mother's suicide note."

Ethan hung his head and said a quick, silent prayer for the girl she'd been, for the woman she'd become.

"And like her mother had all those years earlier, Hope shut herself in her room. Refused to come out for over a week. Now, mind you, she'd been a happy-go-lucky child, despite how stern Alice and John were. Always smiling. Always trying to brighten everyone else's mood."

Picturing Hope's bright face, Ethan had no trouble believing that at all.

"After she came out of her room, she was still pleasant enough, still smiled a lot…but the smile never quite made it to her eyes…."

Like Molly, Ethan thought.

"Then she went away to college. Best thing that could have happened, if you ask me, because when she came home after graduation, Hope seemed more like her old self."

Ethan heard the implication loud and clear. She may have been "more like her old self," but she still wasn't the happy kid she'd been before finding that box in the attic.

It all made sense now—the way she'd fidgeted when he'd showed her around his neat-as-a-pin house, how she'd gasped quietly when he'd taken her into Molly's stark, grown-up room, the way she'd lit up like a Christmas tree when he'd asked her to help him fix up the place for Molly….

Ethan got it now. He knew her special connection with his goddaughter existed because she saw a bit of herself in the little girl's eyes, heard an echo of her own past in the child's silence. No wonder she'd chosen counseling as her profession. *Christian* counseling, no less, specializing in children's needs. He believed she hoped to prove to troubled children that God loved them, gently and tenderly, even when their own parents seemed incapable of doing so.

Ethan felt a jumble of emotions for Hope at that moment—empathy, admiration, respect—but not pity. Her loveliness went far deeper than her big eyes, her shining hair, her delightful smile. She'd worked hard to make something beautiful and redemptive of her ugly and difficult past. And for that, he respected her with all he had, down to the very marrow of his bones.

Hearing her story in a ten-minute time frame all but wiped him out. If his calendar hadn't been packed with back-to-back meetings, he might just have left the office and headed home to take a nap.

No...sleep wasn't what he needed. What he needed was to be with her.

"If everything goes well," he said to Mrs. Cummings, "I'll bring Molly to Sunday school this week. But you'll understand if we can't make it, right?"

"Of course," she said. "*For everything there is a season....*'"

"'...*and a time for every matter under heaven.*'"

He'd always been partial to those verses from Ecclesiastes. And as he hung up the phone, another verse popped into his head—Romans 15:13: "*May the God of hope fill you with all joy and peace in believing, so that by the power of the Holy Spirit you may abide in hope.*"

Hope.

For the first time since he'd brought Molly home, he had a glimmer of hope that she would survive this terrible trauma.

Hope Majors was his newfound inspiration. After all she'd gone through as a kid, if she could blossom into the beautiful woman he'd had lunch with today…well, he could now hope for the same miracle for Molly!

A stab of guilt hit him in the pit of his stomach. He was falling for Hope, hard and fast. But now—now that he knew all she'd suffered and endured without complaint, now that he knew what she'd become, despite the odds—

Don't add to her problems, Burke. A guy like you, who's never around when he's needed…the last thing she needs is somebody else who might let her down. And the sad fact set in that he'd been running from commitment his entire adult life. What made him think he could stop running now?

Maybe enough time had passed. Maybe his life of solitude and loneliness had finally atoned for all the times he'd been absent when those who loved him needed him. Maybe the tide was turning. After all, Sam and Shari had known him for years. Had been privy to every ugly detail of his miserable past. And yet they'd entrusted him with Molly, the closest thing to both their hearts. Would they have done that if they hadn't believed he was fit for the job?

He shook his head.

They'd loved Molly more than life itself. Not in a million years would they have consciously handed her over to someone whom they feared wouldn't be there for her anytime, anyplace, any reason she needed him!

"For everything there is a season…."

Maybe the seasons are changing, Burke. Maybe God's purpose is for you to finally need and be needed, to trust and be trusted, to love and be loved….

He stood at his office window, hands clasped at the small of his back, staring past the sea of cars in the lot below. Hundreds of vehicles were parked down there, all owned by the men and women who'd come to depend on him to provide for them and their families with steady paychecks, health insurance, Christmas bonuses. He owed these people a lot—owed them everything, in fact. And that's why Ethan hadn't missed a day of work, not one, in the eight years since he'd founded the corporation. Whether they'd hired on as employees at one of his hotels, at one of his restaurants, or at any one of the dozens of other companies that were part of Burke Enterprises, they were family. He *liked* taking care of them, providing for them....

It was time to extend that attitude to Molly. Ethan had a long way to go to become the father Sam had been, but he intended to try to fill his shoes.

He wanted to be worthy of Hope, too, because she deserved a warm, welcoming home of her own, filled with children who adored her and a husband who thought she'd single-handedly arranged every star in the sky.

Lord, if You've seen fit to bless me with a daughter like Molly and a woman like Hope, surely You'll bless me with what's lacking in my character...so I'll deserve them.

A light rapping at his door interrupted Ethan's musings. "Yes?"

Kate poked her head into his office. "The graphics guy is here to discuss how you want the corporate brochure laid out this year."

He clapped a hand to the back of his neck. "Okay. Put him in the conference room and get him some coffee, and tell him I'll be there in a minute."

"Headache?" she said as she came further into the room.

"Nah." He started making neat stacks of the paperwork on his desk.

Kate inclined her head and, frowning, grabbed the tablet from the top of one pile. "What's this?"

Ethan's ears got hot suddenly. With sweaty palms, he grabbed the tablet back from the tall, blonde marketing manager. During his conversation with Mrs. Cummings, he'd absentmindedly doodled "Hope" all over the page. The repetitive scrawl reminded him of the time in fourth grade when his teacher had made him write the word *definition* one hundred times to fuse the proper spelling into his brain.

He tossed the pad facedown on his desk, adjusted the knot of his tie, and jutted out his chin. It wasn't easy ignoring Kate's indignant expression, but he managed. "Does Pete know the graphics guy is here?" he asked her.

She pulled herself up to her full six-foot height. "He's already in the conference room," she said, more sharply than necessary.

His embarrassment was cooled by the dawning realization that Kate was angry. Very angry. *What's your problem?* he wanted to say. Instead, he fished around on the desktop for the marketing campaign folder.

"So, are you thinking about buying the Hope Diamond?"

He looked into her narrowed eyes and said, "Hope is the counselor who's working with Molly."

"Ah-ha. So it's true that she's holding sessions in your den...."

He didn't like the direction this was going. Didn't like it one bit. "Kate, I believe we have people waiting?"

Pursing her lips, she turned on her heel and strutted toward the door. "Yes, sir!" she snapped, turning around and saluting. "Whenever you're ready, sir!" And with that, she left the room, slamming the door behind her.

Oh, great, he said to himself, *like you don't already have enough problems.* Kate's behavior only served to accentuate how different Hope was from every other woman he knew. He considered reprimanding Kate's insubordination but thought better of it. He was at least 50 percent to blame for the fact that Kate thought something more existed between them than a business relationship; while he'd never encouraged her behavior, he'd never *discouraged* it, either. He was just shallow enough to enjoy her jealousy a little.

The admission made him wonder if Hope would ever care enough about him to feel jealous of another woman, and the possibility that she wouldn't caused an ache in his heart that reverberated throughout his soul.

Frowning, Ethan gathered his marketing file and a blank notepad and stomped to the conference room, determined to shrug off his mounting feelings of self-pity. He'd never been afraid of taking chances before. Risked everything to turn Burke Enterprises into a Fortune 500 company.

His head and his heart went to war:

She might reject you, said his head.

Maybe, answered his heart.

It'll hurt like the dickens if she does....

No doubt about it.

Think you can survive that? his head taunted.

And his heart responded, *I doubt it.*

He gave a moment's thought to how life might be with a woman like Hope—a woman who'd love him for the man he'd become instead of for the properties he owned. A woman who'd love him and their children completely, no holds barred.

How can you be so sure that's the kind of woman she is? asked his head.

In all honesty, Ethan had no answer for that one. At least, none that made sense, especially considering the short time he'd known her. "She'll be good for Molly and me," he mumbled. "I just *know* it."

He stood outside the conference room door, picturing her warm smile and bright green eyes, which sparkled with a love for life.

Then take the risk, said his heart.

And even before Ethan had seated himself at the head of the long mahogany table, he knew without a doubt that he would.

∽∾

Bright and early Saturday morning, Hope showed up at the appointed time, ready for a day of shopping. She'd worn her favorite sneakers, thick, white socks, slim jeans, and a pastel pink turtleneck sweater. Just in case the weather turned crisp, as it often did in September, she'd slipped into a navy blazer.

As she locked her car door, she had the sense that someone was watching her. Looking up, she saw Ethan on the other side of the parking lot, one hand in his pant pocket, one foot crossed over the other as he leaned against the driver-side door of his low-slung sports car. He threw a hand into the air, and though she couldn't see his eyes behind the mirrorlike lenses of his aviator sunglasses, she could only assume from the width of his smile that he was happy to see her.

How was it possible, Hope wondered, walking toward him, that every time she saw him, he looked more handsome than the time before? Today, he wore crisp jeans and new running shoes, and the red of his long-sleeved golf shirt peeked out from beneath a lightweight bomber jacket. At lunch a few days earlier, she'd noticed how his dark hair had curled over his collar. He'd gotten a haircut....

"Where's Molly?" she asked, walking up to him.

When he nodded toward the car, Hope bent at the waist to peer into the backseat, but the sun's reflection on the tinted glass kept her from seeing inside. Straightening, she frowned. "Did you tell her what we planned to do today?"

"Yeah, I explained," he said dully. "Guess she's not into spending money." Shooting Hope a crooked grin, he added, "She's gonna make some guy a great wife someday if she holds on to that attitude."

She returned his smile. "Funny. Very funny." Walking around to the passenger side of the convertible, she opened the door. "Hey, Molly-girl," she said, "what say you unbuckle that seat belt and come with us so that we can do our best to send your uncle Ethan to the poor house?"

The girl did as she was told, then stood silently beside the car, hands clasped at her waist. To that point, Hope had been feeling pretty chipper, like this little outing might actually be fun. Just two ordinary people taking a preteen girl out for a shopping spree. What could be more normal and natural? But one look at the girl's wooden movements and expressionless face served to remind her just how big a task she and Ethan faced.

Hope sighed and sent a quick prayer heavenward. *Lord, put the right words into my mouth today.* Then, resting a hand on Molly's shoulder, she said, "Did you bring a purse, sweetie?"

No response…unless she chose to count frowning at the pavement as a reaction.

Hope lowered herself to Molly's eye level so that their gazes met. "Well, then, we'll just have to make sure Uncle Ethan gets one for you today, won't we?"

Molly looked straight into Hope's eyes, blinking once or twice before attempting to turn way. But Hope moved her own head accordingly, forcing Molly to continue making eye contact. *Kiddo, you're doing a swell job of acting stubborn, but whether you know it or not, you've just met your match!*

Casting a furtive glance at Ethan, who was leaning against the car and watching them, she smiled. "I hope you ate a good break-fast, because we girls intend to walk your feet off!"

He slid his sunglasses up onto his head. "Two eggs over easy, Canadian bacon, and buttered toast. That'll hold me for a while." Winking, he added, "But keep in mind, I'm six-one—"

"Yeah," she countered, hands on her hips now, "so?"

"So, my legs are longer than yours and Molly's. I think it's you two who'll be hot-footin' it to keep up with me!"

Hope turned to Molly, fully prepared to say, "Did you get a load of that?" But she saw that the girl had indeed been paying close attention to the exchange...

...and was *smiling*!

In an instant, as if she realized a bit of joy had squeaked from her, Molly looked down at the toes of her shoes. Hope glanced up to see if Ethan had noticed the fleeting transformation, too. The look of disappointment on his face told her that he had. She pointed toward the mall entrance. "Inside, Daddy Longlegs," she said in the cheeriest voice she could muster, "'cause we're burnin' daylight!"

Laughing, Ethan joined her and Molly on their side of the car and, taking each of them by the hand, started walking toward the wide glass doors.

Hope's heart beat hard and her pulse pounded as she won-dered if he was squeezing Molly's hand the way he was squeezing hers....

Chapter Six

Whew," Ethan breathed, flopping onto the family room sofa beside Hope. "I'm bushed! How do you do it, with legs as short as yours?"

Hope faced him. "The air is thinner up there where you are, smart guy, so naturally I have an edge." She toed off her shoes and propped both feet on the coffee table, then quickly lifted them. "Uh…it's okay to do that, right?"

His feet joined hers. "The thing is granite, darlin'," he said, chuckling. "It'd take more than those itty-bitty feet of yours to do it any harm."

Several moments of companionable silence passed before she sat up. "I have a confession to make."

"It isn't gonna make me blush, is it?"

"If it does," she said, laughing, "you're *wa-a-ay* too sensitive, Mr. Burke."

"Okay, but I have to warn you, I have no experience with absolution."

Grinning, she sighed. "Not that kind of confession, silly. I was just going to admit I've never actually snuggled into a leather sofa before. It's much more comfortable than I would have guessed."

Both his dark eyebrows rose on his forehead. "Why's that?"

"I guess I thought it would be cold. And that it'd make crackly noises. Like vinyl, y'know, and—"

His smile silenced her. "Okay, so I'm an unsophisticated twit," she said. "Sue me."

"From what I hear, you're plenty sophisticated."

Hope's heart began beating double-time as a flush crept into her cheeks. "What do you mean?"

"Just thinking of what Mrs. Cummings said when I called to enroll Molly in Sunday scho—"

"Mrs. Cummings!" she blurted out, leaping to her feet. "Why, if that old busybody actually knew half of what she professes to know, she'd put the TV news anchors to shame." She didn't want to be pacing, but it seemed she was powerless to make herself stop.

Soon, Ethan was on his feet, too. "Easy, girl," he said, placing his hands on her shoulders. "She thinks the world of you. Told me Molly couldn't be in better hands."

Now she felt like a goof for overreacting that way. "Oh," she said, biting her lower lip. "Sorry. That was a terrible thing to say about the woman. *Terrible!*"

He lifted her chin gently with his forefinger. "No need to apologize. I've known her for a while, too, y'know. And much as I hate to admit it, you're right. The poor old dear is a busybody."

Hope stared into his long-lashed dark eyes for a quiet, intense moment. There was no need to hide her past from him. She could see that in the understanding expression on his handsome face. Which told her he already knew everything. He *knew*, and now he felt sorry for her!

Hope wanted to turn and run. She thought about grabbing her blazer and purse and heading for the door, but the warm hands on her shoulders wouldn't allow it. The steady *ticktock, ticktock, ticktock* of the grandfather clock in the hall counted the seconds. With no warning whatever, Ethan pulled her close. She pressed her cheek to his shirt as the clock went *ticktock, ticktock, ticktock* some more. "She told you, didn't she?" Hope finally asked.

Ethan eased her gently to arm's length and nodded.

Hope's gaze slid toward the windows, then followed the gentle slope of the grassy hillside down to the ebbing river below. A blue heron sailed gracefully by, its wide wings outstretched to catch the crisp autumn wind as it searched for a suitable perch. She watched it disappear from view, wishing she could do the same. Oh, to have freedom like that, to sail off on an air current and leave behind whatever ails you.

Whatever ails you....

Hadn't she said something along those lines the first time she'd visited him here? *Ironic*, she thought, *that you were advising him about seeing the value in what was right under his nose, when it was you who didn't have a clue.*

"Hope?"

She sighed. "Mmm?"

"Does it bother you that I know?"

Maybe what he knows has nothing to do with your mother, or your father, or—

He ran the fingertips of his right hand through her hair as his left thumb drew lazy circles on her jaw. "What happened back then," he began, "had nothing to do with you."

Well, what else could the poor man say? In his shoes, she'd have said something similar.

In his shoes....

Ethan had just admitted that he knew about her miserable past. Maybe all his kindness and compassion were simply to soften

the news that he'd found a more suitable counselor for his traumatized goddaughter.

Until today, Hope had thought she'd outgrown the humiliation of her past. But now, as she stood in the spotlight of his gaze,
she knew she hadn't outgrown it. Probably never would outgrow it.

She hadn't admitted it to herself until now, but Ethan Burke
had come to mean a great deal to her. Despite her "never mix
business with pleasure" motto, she'd found herself hoping he saw
something in her, so that when Molly's condition improved....

Well, fat chance of that happening now. Because now, all she
had was his pity.

"You have to stop holding yourself accountable for—"

He stopped speaking so suddenly that Hope couldn't help but
look up at him. She expected to find the sympathetic expression
still darkening his eyes. But he'd clamped his teeth together so
tightly that his jaw muscles were bulging. His generous mouth
formed a thin, taut line, and his big dark eyes were mere slits.
Didn't take a genius to figure out that he was angry. Very angry.

Was he mad that she hadn't told him more about her history?
He probably would have liked to have found another counselor
to work with Molly—one who hadn't been conceived in sin by a
mother who consequently committed suicide. Did he think her
past would somehow taint the innocent little girl?

"You deserved a lot better than that," he said sternly. "A whole
lot better."

Surely, she was hearing things....

Gently, he pressed a palm to each of her cheeks, his fingertips
combing the hair back from her face. "I don't make a habit of questioning the Almighty," he rasped, "but this is one instance when I can't
help but wonder what inspired Him to give you *those* two for parents."

No question about it…she was hearing things….

"It wasn't *all* their fault," she said, quoting her mantra. "For years, I've believed there must have been something wrong with me, because why else would—?"

"I hope your use of the past tense means you don't still feel that way."

Her eyes met his, and she tried a half grin on for size. "I guess you'd have to say I'm a work in progress. My interest in psychology was rooted in questions about my past. When I went searching for reasons to explain why my parents hadn't loved me, hadn't wanted me, I discovered there were hundreds, even thousands, of kids who felt as I did."

Pastor Cummings, she told Ethan, had taught her many things in his infinite patience, but she held one lesson especially close: No matter what, *God* loved her. It was in His holy Word that Hope had found—for the first time in her life—true acceptance, unconditional love, mercy, understanding, and forgiveness.

"Forgiveness for *what?*" Ethan demanded. "You didn't *do* anything!" He let out a sigh of exasperation. "There's a little girl upstairs who's sleeping soundly on blue sheets with clouds on 'em because you somehow knew she wanted them. And that same little girl smiled today. *Smiled*, Hope. More than once. And you're the reason she did. In three long months, you're the first person who's managed to reach her, and that fact alone is enough to convince me that it'll be you who'll get her to open up all the way."

Ethan gave her another gentle shake and kissed the top of her head. "I've been thanking the good Lord for the past several days that you're here for Molly." He hesitated, then added, "And for me." He pulled her close to him again.

It was a lot to absorb in such a short while, but Hope had a feeling Ethan would give her the time and space she needed to get the job done. Standing in the protective circle of his arms with her ear pressed against his broad chest, she counted the beats of his heart.

And oh, what a big heart it was to have made room for a frightened little girl and a lonely young woman!

All the time they'd been standing this way, she hadn't even minded that his big shoe had been resting on the toe of her sneaker. Nor had she minded that when he'd kissed her head, her hair had somehow gotten tangled in the top button of his shirt.

"Ethan?"

"Hmm?"

"I think we have a problem."

"Nothing we can't solve with God's help."

His response sounded so sincere, so heartfelt, that Hope felt a little guilty about the giggles it inspired.

He tried to step back, no doubt to see what was so funny, and he froze when he realized what had happened. "Well," he said, mimicking Oliver Hardy, "isn't *this* a fine fix you've got us in?" Then, "Scissors are not an option. Anybody who goes near those gorgeous curls has to answer to me." And he punctuated the threat by pressing a kiss to her lips.

When they came up for air, she said, "Um, Ethan?"

This time, a note of suspicion echoed in his "Hmm?"

"We have another problem."

"I'm almost afraid to ask what—"

"You're...standing on my foot."

His attempt to glance down was halted by her hair, still firmly wound up in his button.

"Good gravy." And this time when he stepped back, he took her with him.

"Ouch!"

"Sorry...." With his hands on her shoulders, he looked deep into her eyes, then startled to chuckle deep and loud.

The sound was contagious, and soon the two of them were blotting tears of mirth from their eyes.

⁂

He couldn't very well discuss it in the doorway as he said good night to Hope. Not with Molly standing at the top of the steps, watching them—and giggling behind one hand. It had taken all the willpower Ethan could muster to keep from signaling Hope, but he didn't want to risk pushing Molly further from him by making too big a deal of her laughter.

After waving good-bye to Hope, he gave Molly a minute to scurry back to bed, then headed upstairs to peek in on his goddaughter. It was hard to believe that only this morning, the room had been somber and sedate. The bureau, rolltop desk, and four-poster bed still sat where he'd put them, and Hope had suggested leaving the deep-blue Persian rug on the floor and the wide-slatted blinds in the window. But the maroon valances and square-cut bed skirt were gone, along with the matching comforter.

Earlier, he'd wondered what Hope would do with the yards of gauzy creme-colored stuff she'd purchased at the fabric store, and now he knew. The filmy material hung in graceful billows from the headboard, and she'd flung it over the wooden curtain rods, too, giving the windows a soft, airy look that was feminine and classy... the perfect backdrop for the pale-blue quilt and ruffled pillow shams they'd picked up at the bed and bath shop.

The beady black eyes of two dozen stuffed animals stared at him from their new home on the cushioned window seat, and various board games, sketch pads, watercolor paint sets, and crayons decorated the low round table in the middle of the floor.

Huge silver-framed prints of ballerinas graced the walls. A tall lamp sculpted of white alabaster stood near the desk, and two shorter versions of it sat on the nightstands. A jewelry box adorned the bureau, its open glass lid exposing bangle bracelets, beaded necklaces, and faux gemstone rings. Inside the dresser were outfits Hope had chosen by watching Molly's reaction to every hanger she held up. And in the closet were a winter coat, knee-high boots, half a dozen dresses in assorted colors, and a tidy row of girlie shoes.

Ethan hadn't noticed any change in Molly's expression as the threesome had traipsed from one store to the next, dragging a dozen overflowing shopping bags. "That's because you were standing off to the side," Hope had said. "I had the better vantage point. Besides," she teased, "I'm closer to her size, so it's easier for me to gauge her reaction to things."

Now, he knelt down beside the girl's bed and took another look around the room. Part of Molly's childhood had been restored today, thanks to Hope. Tugging the covers up under her chin, he kissed her cheek. "G'night, sweet girl," he whispered, then tiptoed from the room. And in the doorway, he added, "I love you...."

He was halfway down the stairs when a small, soft voice stopped him dead in his tracks. "I love you, too, Uncle Ethan."

His heart pounding with hope and anticipation, Ethan needed almost no time to retrace his steps. But when he poked his head back into her room, the only thing he heard was Molly's steady, measured breaths, and he did his best to bite back bitter disappointment.

⧉⧉

He stared at his Rolex. Nine twenty-three and fourteen seconds.

Ethan had already called Hope's number twice, though he conceded that it would make no sense for her to have made it home in such a short time. He decided to give her half an hour before trying again. Grabbing a glass of water, he headed for his study. The time was sure to pass quickly if he spent it with his Bible. Hopefully, the Lord would lead him to passages that talked about the word *hope*.

Sure enough, Ethan found verse after verse on the subject, though the first few were about hopelessness. Then he stumbled upon 2 Thessalonians 2:15–17: *"Hold to the traditions which you were taught by us, either by word of mouth or by letter. Now may our Lord Jesus Christ himself, and God our Father, who loved us and gave us eternal comfort and good hope through grace, comfort your hearts and establish them in every good work and word."* As he was about to jot down the Scripture reference for later memorization, the phone rang.

"Hi, there!" Hope said when he answered.

Man, but he loved the sound of her voice!

"I saw on my caller ID that you'd called a few times. Is everything all right?"

Everything is fine now.... "I was just wondering if you'd happened to notice Molly at the top of the stairs as you were leaving?"

"No...."

"I have no idea how long she'd been up there, but it was pretty obvious she'd been watching us."

He heard her quiet gasp.

"Saw her from the corner of my eye," he continued, "and she was grinning from ear to ear."

"Thanks to my hair getting snagged on your button, no doubt." And she punctuated the sentence with a merry giggle.

Ethan looked down at the few curly, coppery strands still clinging to his shirt and thought this one might never make it to the dry cleaner's....

"It's a good sign, Ethan, a very good sign. She made a lot of progress today. Before you know it, she won't need me at all!"

He'd never thought of it quite that way before, but, as usual, she'd hit the proverbial nail right on the head. When Molly was better and had resumed speech, the therapy sessions would end. Much as he wanted a happy, healthy godchild back—and he wanted that more than he could express—he didn't like the idea of less time with Hope. Didn't like it at all. "We'll still want to see a lot of you, though," he said. "I'm going to insist on it."

"Seems an unnecessary expense...."

"Holy cow, Hope. I never imagined you were so mercenary that you'd charge for friendship. Maybe I should bring you on board at Burke Enterprises. We can always use another hungry shark!"

She laughed along with him. "Say, does your company have a day-care program?"

"No," he admitted. "I'm ashamed to say I never even gave one a thought. Maybe when we get Molly squared away, you'll help me with that...?"

He heard her yawn. "I'd love to," she said around it.

"Well, I'd better let you go. You worked your pretty little fingers to the bone today. I'm sure you're exhausted."

"It was a hoot. I loved every minute."

"I still can't believe all you accomplished in just one day. You're a regular whirling dervish. A cyclone. A tornado. A—"

"You sure know how to turn a girl's head," she said, laughing. "Is that your gentlemanly way of telling me I'm just a lot of wind?"

"Is that what I did, Hope?" When she didn't respond, he added, "Did I turn your head?"

The ensuing silence was so long, so deafening, that he thought maybe they'd been disconnected. Or that she'd hung up.... Then, in a quiet, tentative voice, she said, "I don't know why you'd want to, but it's turned. Definitely."

Now he understood what the poets meant when they wrote about soaring hearts and singing souls. Ethan couldn't remember hearing better news.

"What about you?" she asked.

"What about me?"

"Is your head turned?"

"Like a hoot owl's! I'll have you know I've been walkin' into walls, thanks to you."

"I'm flattered," she said. Just then, he heard her doorbell ring in the background. "Now, who can that be at this hour?"

His free hand involuntarily formed a fist. "I'll hang on while you see who it is. And I'll call the cops if I hear anything that makes it seem somebody's up to no good."

"The deadbolt is in place, and I have a peephole. See you and Molly tomorrow!"

"Right." He didn't want to let her go. "Tomorrow."

This time when the bell sounded, it was clear the person on the other side of the door had grown impatient waiting for her to answer it. "I'd better go."

"Right. Sorry." He swallowed. "Hope?"

"Yes...?"

"Will you call me when the nutball who's trying to wear out your doorbell at midnight goes away...so I won't worry?"

Soft laughter filtered into his ear. "It's only nine thirty...."

"But you'll call?"

"If it isn't too late."

What did that mean? "Doesn't matter what time it is...."

"I really have to go, Ethan. See you tomorrow," she said, and hung up.

Ethan stared at the receiver until its buzzing sound prompted him to put it back into its cradle. He'd never been this way—possessive, protective, sentimental—with a woman before. Not with actresses or fashion models or corporate executives. So what was this crazy behavior all about?

"You're losin' your mind, Burke," he said, trudging toward the kitchen. Then, staring at the spot on the floor where he'd found her earring, he grinned. "Well, if you're gonna lose it, you might as well be with someone who can help you find it."

Chapter Seven

Hope immediately recognized the distinguished-looking gentleman at her door, because she'd seen his photograph on the mantle in Ethan's family room. But why would his father visit her unannounced at this hour? And how had he found her?

"Mr. Burke," she said, opening the door, "what can I do for you?"

"Please, please," he said, "call me Sawyer. Mr. Burke was my father's name!" He gave a hearty laugh and, despite the fact that she hadn't invited him to do so, stepped inside. "Nice place you've got here," he said, looking around the living room. "Lived here long?"

She closed the door and joined him near the coffee table. "Two years this Thanksgiving."

Ethan had apparently inherited his strikingly good looks from his mother's side of the family, because there was no physical resemblance between Sawyer Burke and his son.

The smile in the older man's eyes dimmed as he ran a hand through his silvery hair…the first similarity to Ethan that she'd seen. "I'll be blunt, Miss Majors," he said. "This isn't a social call."

Hope tucked the fingertips of both hands into the back pockets of her jeans, wondering why on earth he *was* here. Lifting her chin a notch, she said, "I'm not surprised. You seem too much a gentleman to drop in so late, uninvited."

"Touché," he said. "Do you suppose I could bother you for a cup of tea while I tell you why I'm here?" He rubbed his hands together. "It's a mite brisk out there, and I'm afraid these old bones don't take to the cool weather like they used to."

Old? Other than the thick, snow-white hair, he could easily have passed for fifty. "Of course," she said. "The kitchen's right this way."

She was standing at the sink filling the teapot with water when he said, "You know, I had a feeling I was going to like you."

Hope shot a glance over her shoulder as he added, "And I was right."

What an odd thing to say, she thought, more curious than ever to learn what he could possibly want to talk about with her. She set the copper kettle on a front burner of the stove. "Please don't think me rude," she said, firing up the flame, "but it's getting late and—"

"I'll get right to the point, then," he said, taking a seat at the table. "I'm worried about Ethan. Very worried."

She dropped two tea bags into two red ceramic mugs, thinking that Ethan was the most in-charge-of-himself man she'd ever met. He was the last guy she'd think to arouse concern in his father. "What's the problem?"

"That child he's brought home with him is—"

"You mean Molly?"

"Yes. Of course. Forgive me. It's just that Molly is a reminder of some terrible times in my boy's past. With everything else that's on his shoulders these days, I just wonder if he can handle the extra pressure...and the memories."

She filled the mugs with steaming water and carried them to the table. "What memories?"

Sawyer frowned. "I'm afraid that in order to understand Ethan—and you'll need to do just that if the two of you hope to help that little girl—I'm going to have to tell you a few things about myself." He cleared his throat and spooned some sugar into his cup. "Some rather...uh, unsavory things, I'm afraid."

"I feel I should point out that I'm *Molly's* counselor, not Ethan's." *Or yours*, she tacked on mentally.

"I'm well aware of that. He told me all about you when I stopped by to see him yesterday." The man gave a knowing little nod. "He depends on you far more than you know."

"Because of the work I'm doing with Molly."

"There's that, of course, but what he feels for you isn't entirely because of the child."

Hope didn't know how to respond to that, and so she said nothing. But her mind whirled.... Ethan, who ran a multimillion-dollar corporation, who employed thousands of employees, whose neighbors were rich and famous...*that* man depended on her?

"Since it's clear you're going to be a part of his life," his father continued, "there are a few things you should know. To help you help him...and Molly."

"I don't know how big a part I'll play in *his* life," she confessed, "once Molly is better."

"I know my son very well, Hope—though I'm sure he'd tell you otherwise—and I can assure you that you've become a very important part of his life." He chuckled, reminding her again of his son. "Why, I wouldn't be the least bit surprised, in a month or two, to hear that he's popped the question."

Hope swallowed a gasp. She liked Ethan. Liked him a lot. And if that kiss in his family room had been any indicator, he liked her, too. But marriage? A nervous giggle popped from her mouth. "Really, Mr. Burke, I—"

"Sawyer, remember?" Another chuckle. "Or maybe you should practice calling me Dad."

She felt a blush creep into her cheeks. "Would you like me to warm up your tea?"

"Ah, a diplomat, I see," he said, winking. "In the line of work he's in, he needs a woman like you at his side."

It was ridiculous—no, ludicrous—to consider anything he was saying as logical! Still....

Sawyer cleared his throat. "Now then, I'll be as brief as possible...."

Too late for that, she thought.

He leaned forward, folded both hands on the tabletop, and took a deep breath. "Did you know Ethan had a younger sister?"

She shook her head. "Had?"

Sawyer nodded. "She died when she was twenty and Ethan was twenty-four. Hard to believe," he said, his voice softening thoughtfully, "that it's been twelve years...."

Hope found herself leaning forward with curiosity. "How did it happen?"

From the look of desperation that shadowed his face, she knew nothing gentle had ended his daughter's life.

"Fire," he rasped.

"Oh, Mr. Burke, that's just awful. I'm so sorry!"

"Yes, awful. Especially considering Ethan blames himself for it."

"But—but why?"

He inhaled a deep, shaky breath, then slowly released it. "Bess was wheelchair-bound and mostly deaf when the, uh...when the fire happened." He shook his head. "And Ethan blames himself for *that*, too." His eyes met hers. "And I'm here to tell you that I'm the reason he blames himself for both.

"You see, by the time Ethan was fourteen, he'd grown pretty tired of having a ten-year-old shadow. His friends teased him because he couldn't go anywhere without Bess on his heels. The two of them had gone to summer camp together from the time Bess was four, and, naturally, Ethan couldn't have fun with his little sister hanging around all the time.

"So when he turned fourteen, he insisted he was too old for 'kid stuff' and refused to go to camp at all." Sawyer hung his head. "His mother and I saw no reason to make him go if he didn't want to, so that year, Bess went alone...."

The way his voice trailed off gave Hope a sinking feeling. She took a sip of tea and waited for him to continue.

"One rainy morning, she was running along the pier. She'd been told to stay inside, but Bess had a mind of her own. She tripped and fell into the pond." Wincing, Sawyer rubbed his face with both hands. "She hit her back on the edge of the decking, damaging her spinal cord. And she stayed underwater long enough to incur a three-quarter hearing loss."

He was frowning hard now and staring into his cup, as if he could see on the mirrorlike surface of the tea a rerun of that day. "When Bess regained consciousness in the hospital, she was para- lyzed form the waist down."

Hope hung her head, feeling guilty for the judgmental thoughts she'd entertained about this man only moments ago. "I'm sorry, Sawyer."

He took a deep, shuddering breath. "Yes, well, such is life, right? But I'm afraid that isn't the worst of it." And, driving both hands through his hair, the man said, "In the hospital, I pinned Ethan against the wall. 'Are you satisfied?' I asked him. 'You couldn't be bothered to mind your little sister, and now look at her!'"

Hope's eyes widened as she wondered how he could have said such a thing.

"Believe me, I've asked myself ten thousand times how I could have said a horrible thing like that." A quiet moment passed before he added, "Then, from the moment we brought her home from the hospital, Ethan became *Bess's* shadow. He learned sign language and taught it to her. Taught her to read lips, too." He drained his cup and wrapped trembling hands around it. "And his mother and I, we let him. I spent less and less time at home. Got myself tangled up with a young woman whom I thought would help me forget all the miserable aspects of my life and—"

She saw the tears in his eyes and blanketed his hands with her own. "Sawyer, there's really no need to tell me all of this. I—"

"There's every need!" he all but hollered. "I have to make you understand, so you can help him. I owe him that much, at least!"

She sat back, stunned into silence by his outburst. Then, she said softly, "The Lord doesn't hold you responsible for what happened to Bess, and I'm sure Ethan doesn't, either."

Ethan's father harrumphed. "But that's just it, don't you see? He holds *himself* responsible, because when he was little more than a boy, I told him he *was* responsible."

Slipping his hands from beneath hers, he ran a fingertip around the rim of his cup. "Tragedy sometimes brings people together, makes them closer. Not my wife and me. I left Ethan's mother about a year after Bess came home from the hospital. Bought a little house on the river so I could be near the kids.... She died before the divorce was even final."

Hope wanted to ask how, to find out what had happened to Ethan's mother, but she held her silence.

"I insisted the doctors tell the kids she'd had a heart attack. Couldn't bear to heap the truth on them, after all they'd already suffered." He met her eyes. "Overdose," he said flatly. "Thankfully, I found the note before anyone else could...and burned it."

Hope had promised to call Ethan when her late-night visitor had left. But how could she do that now? What would she say? *Your father was here, and oh, the stories he—*"

"So I sold the little house on the river and moved back in with the kids. And one night after they'd gone to bed, I went up to check on them and heard crying from Bess's room.

"It was Ethan—just sixteen at the time—on his knees beside her bed, praying with everything God gave him. She couldn't hear a word of it, of course, so I suppose he figured he was safe making his confession. And if I live to be a thousand," he said on a ragged note, "I'll never forget what that boy said...."

Sawyer closed his eyes and quoted his then teenage son: "'I'll take care of you, Bess,' he said. 'Always and forever, to make it up to you. I'll never leave you alone again. I promise.'"

No wonder Ethan had donated millions to children's charities. No wonder he'd built a burn unit at Bayview Medical Center and opened a long-term care facility for handicapped kids. Hope's heart ached for him—for the anguished boy he'd been, for the generous man he'd become.

It came to her in a flash. No *wonder* Molly's recovery was so important to him! Somehow, she believed, he'd found a way to blame himself for every tragedy in his life and had talked himself into believing Sam and Shari's accident had been his fault.

"He kept that promise," Sawyer went on. "Spent every spare moment right there beside her for years. Then, one day, while I was at work...."

Hope shuddered, remembering he'd said a fire had ended Bess's life.

"The neighbors told me they heard the kids arguing down by the pool. Bess wanted to go up to the house for a bowl of soup, and when Ethan wouldn't let her, she got furious and signed to say she wasn't a baby, and that he was making her miserable with his over-protectiveness. She told him if he loved her, he'd prove it by letting her do things for herself. So he did. And somehow, her clothes caught fire, and before he knew what was happening...."

He heaved a final coarse sigh and rubbed his eyes with his knuckles. "Well, there you have it, Hope. The whole sad and ugly Burke family saga." He forced a bitter laugh. "After hearing that, I don't know why you'd want any part of us—least of all me—but at least now you can make a decision based on facts. All of them."

She didn't know where he'd gotten the idea that marriage was a foregone conclusion for her and Ethan. Didn't understand why he felt that telling this tale would change her mind, one way or the other, even if a wedding was on the horizon. Not that it mattered. She'd already acknowledged that her feelings for Ethan had gone well beyond the bounds of "strictly professional."

So many things about Ethan made sense to her now—for starters, the way he pampered Molly and did things for her...from a distance. He was terrified that by getting too close, he might somehow put her in harm's way.

Ethan had accomplished so much in his life, and rather than hoard his millions, he willingly shared his wealth with those less fortunate. And now that she knew all he'd suffered and survived... well, Hope admired him all the more.

"Think you can handle him?" Sawyer asked.

She looked into his eyes and said, "I'm not sure, but I want to try."

Sawyer got to his feet and walked into the living room, and Hope stood up to see him out. At the front door, he pulled Hope into a fatherly embrace. "Thank You, God," he breathed into her ear, "thank You!" And, holding her at arm's length, he said, "I have a lot to make up for, and for *years* I've been praying He'd send someone to rescue Ethan from himself." He glanced up at the ceiling and chuckled. "Sure took You long enough!" When he looked at her again, he said, "So tell me, Hope, how does it feel to be the answer to a prayer?"

"Um, can I get back to you on that?"

"I wonder if your mother had any idea when she named you how well the name would fit."

She'd always just accepted that Hope was her name without wondering why or how it had been chosen. And now, she thought maybe she knew.

Chapter Eight

As Sawyer buttoned his jacket to go out, Hope's telephone rang. "Go ahead and get that," he said. "I can let myself out."

Maybe Ethan's dad *had* made a few mistakes—some terrible ones—but they were in the past. Clearly, he'd become a different man. A changed man. A *good* man whose concern for his son's happiness and well-being had driven him out into the night, alone, to confess his sins to a total stranger.

He pressed a quick, fatherly kiss to Hope's cheek as the phone rang again. "Seriously," he said, smiling, "answer it, will you, before the ringing drives me mad?" And with that, he was gone.

She'd barely uttered hello into the kitchen phone when Ethan said, "You *said* you'd call."

"I know, but...." How much should she tell him about her conversation with his dad? Should she tell him anything at all? "I–I...."

"Don't tell me your late-night guest is still there...."

"No—just left." The father-son relationship was already strained, and the last thing Hope wanted was to create more tension between them by telling him who her guest had been...and why he'd stopped by. At least, not before she had a chance to pray about it. "So, are you and Molly going to church tomorrow?"

"Yeah, of course," he said. "I talked with Mrs. Cummings about enrolling Molly in Sunday school, but I forgot to ask what time it starts."

"Nine, and so does the adult Bible study, followed by services at eleven. Think it'll be a help to Molly if I meet you two out front and walk her to the first class?" "That'd be great." A pause, and then, "You locked up after your...uh, company left, right?"

She peeked around the kitchen door. "Not yet, but I'll get it when—"

"Do me a favor," he interrupted her, "and lock it now, will you? I'll hold on."

Oh, you will, will you? she thought, mildly annoyed by the way he seemed to think it was perfectly all right to order her around. But Hope put the phone down with a *clunk* and did as he had asked. "There," she said, picking it up again. "Done. Are you happy now?"

She didn't know what to make of the long silence that followed her question. Had he hung up?

"Very happy. In fact, I'm happier than I've been in a very long time."

Hope chewed her bottom lip. Could Sawyer have been right when he'd said Ethan had begun to care about her as more than Molly's therapist? Did his kiss signal a complete alteration in his intentions? Like it or not—and the professional side of her did not—Hope's heart fluttered in response to the possibility.

"Well, now that I know you're all safe and sound, I'll say good night."

"G'night."

"Sleep tight."

"Don't let the bedbugs bite." A yawn concluded her remark.

"Like Maria would allow a bug in this house!"

And the last thing she heard before the phone started buzzing was the music of his deep, delicious laughter.

◈

Ethan wandered the quiet house for what seemed like an hour, hands in his pockets and head down. Where had this *jealousy* come from? He had no proof that her guest had been a man. But even if it had been, what right did he have to feel this way about it? Besides, if the guy meant anything to her, why had she invited *him* to church in the morning?

Logic raised its ugly head and told him she'd made the offer on Molly's behalf, not his, and his heart sank a little.

He turned on the TV and found and old black-and-white war movie. His hope was that the noise and action would distract him from thoughts of her. Despite the mayhem of cannon blasts and gunfire, he felt calm and serene, for her image floated in front of his face, and he saw instead the way she'd looked setting out napkins, cream and sugar, and teaspoons at his house the other night like a housewife on a 1950s television show.

Had she flitted round her kitchen setting out cookies, pouring tea, and making sure everything was just right for her recent guest, too?

Rubbing his eyes, he forced the question from his mind. Far better to think about the other night when she was bustling around *his* kitchen. "You cooked supper," she'd said, "so I'll clean up." When he'd failed at talking her out of it, Ethan had sat down again at the table, marveling that anyone could take such delight in mundane chores. It made him start to fantasize about life with a woman like that—a woman who took joy in doing little things for the people she cared about, who refused to do anything halfway, from arranging the placemats on the table to folding the dish towel after putting the last of the pots into the cupboard.

Not a woman like that, he thought now, *but that woman.…*

He pictured the room she'd redecorated for Molly and thought of the little girl who, last time he checked, was sleeping contentedly on sheets of blue skies and clouds because of Hope's intervention. How much better would it be for Molly, when she fully recovered from the trauma of losing her parents, if someone like Hope was around, day in and day out, to see to her every need?

Molly had rarely met his eyes since arriving in the U.S., but as the counselor had been tucking the girl in, planting a kiss on her forehead, and wishing her sweet dreams, Molly had looked long and deep into Hope's.

His gaze slid around the family room to the spot where they'd been standing when he'd taken her in his arms and she'd melted against him. He'd taken a long look at the two of them, thanks to the reflection in the French doors to the patio. How good they'd looked together. How *right*. In the glass of the door, he had seen that she'd lifted her face to look at his, so he'd turned to meet her gorgeous green eyes…and had kissed her.

Just thinking about it took his breath away, and, shaking his head, Ethan chuckled to himself. Did she have any idea how captivating she was? Not likely. He might have kissed her a second time, and then a third, if he hadn't seen Molly hugging the newel post at the top of the stairs and grinning like a cat that had swallowed a canary.

One of the reasons he'd been able to turn a one-man, home-based company into a multimillion-dollar corporation was that he'd quickly learned to take the measure of the men he did business with. He had a feeling that if a man was lucky enough to work his way into that big heart of Hope's, he'd be there for life.

Better watch yourself, bud, he thought, *or you could drown in her—Drown.*

He shuddered involuntarily at the word and prayed it would quickly flee from his mind.

In his bedroom, he kicked his sneakers to the back of his closet, draped his shirt over the arm of the big leather chair, and hung his jeans on the closet doorknob. The decorative pillows Maria arranged so artfully every morning thumped softly to the floor as he slid between clean, white sheets.

First, he praised God for allowing him to witness Molly's mischievous grin. Then, he thanked Him for a home that stood on a solid foundation and for the successful company that guaranteed he and his employees could keep their pantries stocked. *And if I dream tonight,* he added, *let me dream of Hope.*

❦

Ethan dove into the lake headfirst and swam as fast as his legs would propel him. Bess was there, right there, just a few yards ahead. He could do this. He could get there, could pull her out of the pond and carry her to safety.

Her brown eyes were wide with fright as her long, dark hair snaked around her head like the fronds of their mother's Boston fern. Kicking frantically, she reached for him, and he could see her lips silently calling his name: "Eeeee-thannn…."

The dainty gold ring he'd given her for her birthday last year caught a beam of sunlight that pierced the depths. Almost there, he told himself, almost there…. Four kicks, then two more, and he'd be near enough to wrap his arms around her and then swim to the surface so she could fill her lungs with life-saving air.

He reached out, felt her fingers graze his, then watched helplessly as she drifted backward, floating farther, sinking deeper, out of his reach.

And the harder he kicked, it seemed, the greater the distance grew between them. A terrified expression was on her face as iridescent bubbles escaped her mouth and rose to the surface, where Bess would be now if he'd been there to keep her from falling into the water in the first place.

He had to get to her, simply had to, because she'd always relied on him, always—

Ethan sat up with a start and sucked in a huge gulp of air. His heart pounding, he glanced around—at the bureau, the windows, the wall hanging that concealed his flat-screen TV, the clothes he'd worn today, scattered here and there…. As he consciously loosed his death grip on his pillow, he saw that he'd kicked the bedclothes into a tangle around his legs. He flopped back onto the pillows and willed himself to take slow, even breaths.

When he was fourteen and fifteen, that dream had tormented him nearly every night. It had come to the point that he would rather have done just about anything than fall asleep and risk a rerun. Before Bess's accident, he'd been a decent student. But afterward? All-nighters had helped him get onto the dean's list, marking period after marking period. And by the time he'd turned sixteen, Ethan had read nearly every book in his mother's extensive collection.

It had been many months since the last time he'd had the dream, because he'd learned that prayer kept the horrible images at bay. But tonight, when he'd asked the Lord to bless his night with dreams of Hope, he'd forgotten to ask Him to keep the nightmare away.

The dim, blue numerals of the clock on his bedside table said 2:43. He'd been down this road enough times to know that sleep would elude him until the alarm buzzed at 5:30, so he slapped the Off button and headed down to his study, stopping in the kitchen for a glass of water on the way.

Settling into his armchair, he allowed his Bible to fall open to a random page, and he read aloud the first verse his gaze settled upon: Mark 10:14. *"But when Jesus saw it he was indignant, and said to them, "Let the children come to me, do not hinder them; for to such belongs the kingdom of God.""*

Ethan could only shake his head in awe, for it had been Bess's favorite passage. He could almost see her sitting at the front of the church and signing it for the two other deaf children in the congregation. *"Truly, I say to you, whoever does not receive the kingdom of God like a child shall not enter it,"* he read on in verse 15.

Marking the page with his thumb, Ethan closed the Good Book as tears welled up in his eyes and sobs shook him.

⊰⊱

For the nearly four months since her mother and father had died, Molly knew that her uncle Ethan had been trying.

Trying to make her feel welcome in his home.

Trying to help her come to grips with the horrible accident.

Trying himself to cope with the loss of his best friends, quickly, so he could devote himself to being the kind of parent he thought she deserved.

Trying to encourage her to tell him why she'd decided never, ever to talk again.

None of it had surprised her.

Molly didn't suppose that most girls her age knew much about things like honor and character, but she'd been hearing about her dad's best friend for as long as she could remember, and because words like *moral, ethical,* and *devoted* had been central to many discussions about her uncle Ethan, it seemed a good idea to look them up in the big *Webster's Dictionary* in the family room to find out what they meant.

Besides, if her daddy had thought Uncle Ethan was "good to the bone," as he'd so often said, then it must be true. And even if her dad hadn't thought the world of him, Molly still would have loved the gentle giant.

She remembered the time when she'd waited until the last minute to work on a science report. The result? A messy, inaccurate paper that earned her a low C. And when Uncle Ethan had seen it, he'd pulled her to him in a sideways hug and said, "Molly, m'girl, every time we do a thing, we leave our mark on it, so it's important to make sure that when folks see the mark *you've* left, they'll have no choice but to say, 'That Molly Sylvester, she always does her best!'"

If she hadn't loved him so, she probably would have shrugged it off. But she'd heard her dad say things like that—about Uncle Ethan—and she wanted nothing more than to hear him praise her that way, too.

Uncle Ethan had been doing his best ever since the double funeral for Molly's parents. And she knew that although he was the kind of man who seemed content to make rules, if someone didn't feel duty bound to follow them, he'd simply shrug and say, "Everybody has to live with the consequences of his choices." Molly understood only too well that this was the reason he hadn't been forceful or pushy about getting answers out of her.

He had a funny way of teaching lessons, and he wasn't anything like most other adults in that way. When he was visiting Molly and her parents at their flat in London, if her parents sent her to bed without dessert because she hadn't finished her chores, Uncle Ethan would always sneak cookies into her room when he came in to say good night. "Only *you* know if you've really earned them or not, and if you haven't, they won't taste good," he would say. It had taken just one bite of one cookie to discover just how right he'd been....

She knew full well that it was mostly her fault that he looked so sad standing beside her bed every night, saying the prayers solo that she used to say right along with him. If only she could tell him how much she loved him, how much she wanted to recite the words with him! Maybe then his dark eyes wouldn't fill with tears and....

Tonight, she remembered, right before he had tucked her in, Uncle Ethan had gone into her bathroom because she'd forgotten to turn out the light. "What's this?" he had asked, his deep voice echoing in the huge, tiled space.

If she'd known he'd go in there, Molly might have done a better job of hiding the figurine. She'd have buried it under a layer of tissues, or in some of the drawing paper Miss Majors had given her.

She thought Maria would be the only one who might ever find the shattered remnants of the adorable porcelain girl. And Maria, always smiling and happy, would naturally assume Molly had accidentally knocked the statue from its shelf....

"What happened?" Uncle Ethan had wanted to know, frowning as he stared down into the wastebasket. Then, he'd returned to her bedside and had gently taken her face in his hands, forcing her to look into his eyes. And she'd thought for sure he'd seen the truth written on her soul.

Oh, how she wished she could have thrown her arms around his neck and let him hug her, and oh, how she wanted to hug him right back! She'd wanted to tell him everything, wanted to answer all of his questions.

But she couldn't.

Because Molly believed she didn't deserve to talk—not ever again. And she didn't deserve nice things, either, like the beautiful Hummel figurines her parents had bought for her birthday every year. "You're such a big girl now," her mom had said, "and we know how well you take care of your things."

"That's right," her dad had agreed, "and that's why we're giving you an early start on the collection you've been wanting...."

But Molly believed she hadn't been a good girl. Hadn't been a nice girl, either. And she hadn't needed a better reason than that to smash the Hummel.

Uncle Ethan seemed so sad, so confused, looking at the splintered remains of the first figurine her parents had given her. "A little Hummel family," they'd said after she'd unwrapped it, "just like ours!"

She hated seeing him this way, but Molly couldn't tell him that it was *her* fault he'd lost his best friends, and she'd lost her mother and father....

Because she'd made a promise and intended to keep it.

Chapter Nine

No way this was an accident," Ethan said. "If the Hummel had fallen, there might have been a few pieces of it in the trash can, but this…it's as if the thing was pulverized."

From the moment she picked up the phone, Hope could hear the distress and fear in Ethan's voice. It had always been part of her job description to treat family members as well as the children in her care, and so she assumed her "competent counselor" voice. "I'm sure there's another explanation," she said, "because Molly doesn't strike me as the type of child who'd deliberately destroy something so precious to her." But if she had, it meant Hope had a lot more work to do with the girl, she realized.

"If there's a reason, I'd sure like to hear it."

"We'll get to the bottom of it."

But he seemed not to have heard her. "It's as though she whacked it with a hammer or something."

"Hmm," she said, trying to raise his spirits, "the case of the pummeled Hummel…."

It took him a moment to react to her feeble attempt at humor. "Ha," he said. "A comedian counselor."

Did he think she was making light of the event? "I can hear that you're upset, Ethan, but I assure you, during our next session, I'll get to the bottom of it."

"Sorry. Guess I make too much out of anything that relates to Molly."

That wasn't the impression she wanted him to get, either! "You're doing a wonderful job with her. Your patience and dedication merit a parenting medal. Believe me, I've seen stress drive moms and dads to the point of going ballistic when things like this happen. Your tenacity astounds me."

"So," he said, "you're saying I'm a patient patient?"

She laughed a little. "I suppose one bad joke deserves another."

"I just wish the Hummel figurine was the first thing I've found...broken."

"What?" Her heartbeat accelerated. "What else have you found?

"Clothes torn, toys broken, stuffed animals destroyed...all things Sam and Shari gave her." He exhaled a long, shuddering sigh. "I don't get it, Hope. I just don't get it."

"How many times has this happened?"

"Over the past two or three weeks, I'd say eight, maybe ten times."

If only she'd thought to ask him earlier if anything of this nature had been going on between her visits with Molly. Her whole plan for therapy would have been different if she'd known—

"I should have told you earlier," he said, as if reading her thoughts. "At first, I chalked it up to ordinary wear and tear, since the things were all a few years old. But when she took to hiding the stuff...."

Hope listened as he described the way he'd found the dolphin Sam had carved for Molly from a piece of driftwood under the dock near the Potomac—minus its dorsal fin. And the sweater Shari had knitted for her, partially unraveled, in the kitchen trash.

Sighing, she rested her forehead on a fist. This wasn't good. Not good at all. Picking up a pencil, she drummed her desk with its eraser. "Anything else you've neglected to tell me?"

Ethan cleared his throat. "I didn't neglect to tell you," he said, a defensive note raising his voice a notch. "The incidents were spaced apart at first, and seemed like...like innocent accidents."

Was he really so divided—running Burke Enterprises and monitoring Molly's daily activities—that he hadn't recognized the seriousness after the second episode? "Innocent accidents? An unraveled sweater and a broken carving, deliberately hidden? Come on, Ethan, get real!" She blew a stream of air through her lips. "Every time we've spoken, whether in person or by phone, what was the very first question I asked you?"

A second of silence ticked by before he droned, "If I've noticed anything out of the ordinary."

She sighed again. "And you honestly didn't see those acts of rage as peculiar—"

"Listen, missy," he interrupted, "there's no need to take that tone with me. *You're* the expert, for cryin' out loud. Why didn't you warn me what to look for? If I'd known she could start bustin' up the furniture, I might have seen it sooner."

"I told you at the start of my work with Molly that I'll do whatever it takes to help my kids. So if my tone upsets you, well, I'm sorry. But you hired me to help your godchild, not to baby *you*."

"Let's get one thing straight," he steamed. "Before my Molly became another one of your *cases*, I told you I'd do anything to help her, which is why I chose you instead of another of the hundreds of children's therapists in the area. Maybe...maybe I—"

Was he about to say maybe he'd made a mistake? That he was thinking of finding someone else? Someone older, or someone who'd racked up more cases during her years in the field? Being fired wouldn't bother Hope if she didn't know with absolute certainty how bad it would be for Molly, who'd finally started making progress and whose behavior proved she was, at last, beginning to trust Hope.

Hope had overstepped her bounds with Ethan just now because she'd overlooked an important detail in the case. He was right. She *should* have given him a list of things to be on the lookout for. She'd mentally accused him of being too distracted by business to notice the danger signs...but *she'd* allowed herself to become distracted—by her feelings for Ethan.

She couldn't afford to alienate him now. Molly's recuperation depended on consistency and steadfastness. "I owe you an apology," she began, "for not being more professional. What I said, the way I said it, was completely uncalled for, and I'm sorry. It won't happen again, I assure you."

"The only assurance I need from you is that you won't jump to conclusions in the future. I know what you're thinking—that I haven't spent enough time with her, that if I had, I might have realized the seriousness of—"

"No more blanket assumptions," she promised.

"The truth is, I don't *know* the difference between acceptable 'acting out' and dangerous behavior. Until Molly was foisted on me, my experience was limited to handing out presents at birthdays and Christmases. I wouldn't know a childhood disorder if it bit me on the nose."

It couldn't have been easy for a man like him—especially considering his background—to admit a thing like that. So why did her brain fixate on the word *foisted?*

As though he'd read her mind, Ethan blurted, "And, please, don't jump on your analysis bandwagon, judging every word that comes out of my mouth. I didn't mean that the way it sounded. I hope you know that."

But did she?

On the one hand, he'd overcome numerous obstacles to get to London immediately after the accident and had done everything humanly possible to make a good home for Molly. On the other hand, his whole life had been turned upside down. No more parties, no more black-tie balls, no more glamorous ladies on his arm at charity functions…because an emotionally distraught little girl had been *foisted* on him.

Ethan sighed heavily. "Listen, I have a meeting in five minutes. I know what that sounds like, believe me, but she's in good hands for the little while it'll take to get things taken care of." A pause, and then, "You're still coming over tonight for Molly's session, right?"

"Of course I am. What gave you the idea I wouldn't be?"

In place of an answer, he asked, "And you'll stay for supper, right?"

"Putting Molly at ease is of paramount importance. She's come to expect that, so it's not a good idea to deviate from— "

"See you at seven, then."

He didn't wait for a reply but simply hung up, leaving Hope to stare in dumbfounded silence at the buzzing receiver. *How have things gotten so out of control?* she wondered. They'd been getting along so well. She'd connected with him better than with any parent before him.

But then, she'd never been kissed by a patient's father before.

And she'd never kissed *back*.

She remembered how his big, strong arms had wrapped around her, and the way he'd looked into her eyes as no man before him had.

It had happened nearly four weeks ago, and Ethan hadn't made a single attempt to kiss her again. She took a deep breath, exhaled it slowly. Obviously, he'd realized the inappropriateness of their developing relationship even before she had, and he'd decided to call an immediate halt to it before it interfered with Molly's treatment.

Molly.

Right now, her feelings were all that mattered.

So Hope swallowed the ache in her throat and tidied the files on her desk. From here on out, she'd guard her reactions to Ethan. Not as much as a handshake would transpire between them. Yes, she'd do the right thing.

But that didn't mean her heart would be in it.

After an uncomfortably quiet supper, Hope led Molly into Ethan's office, where they had been conducting most of their sessions. Closing the door, she waited for Molly to sit down in the chair opposite hers, then she sat down and scooted forward until their knees practically touched. "Your uncle Ethan tells me he's been finding some strange things around the house."

The girl didn't normally make eye contact, but when Hope began listing the peculiar occurrences, she looked up.

"Who are you so angry with, Molly? Are you mad at your mom and dad for leaving you?"

She watched the child's dark eyebrows draw together in a serious frown and knew that if she didn't act fast—while she had Molly's attention—she might never get another chance like this. "Are you upset with them for dying, and forcing you to come here to live with your uncle Ethan? Is that why you're destroying every gift they ever gave you, one by one? Is that how you're punishing them for abandoning you?"

Molly blinked and clenched her teeth.

"I've also noticed you haven't been eating much lately. And your uncle Ethan and Maria have noticed it, too."

Now Molly frowned and crossed both arms over her chest.

Leaning forward, Hope rested her hands on Molly's knees. "You can behave like a stubborn mule if you want to, but it won't get you very far. And do you know why?"

She shook her head and stared at her hands, now fidgeting in her lap.

"Because I'm *way* more mule-headed than you are. Plus, I'm older. And I've had a lot more practice at being stubborn." She leaned down, forcing Molly to see her smile. "Just keep that in mind."

The girl's chin lifted a bit. "I can be more stubborn than you any day!"

That her first words were as a challenge was a good sign. *Let the games begin!* Hope thought. "I want you to know something, Molly Marie Sylvester...."

The pupils of Molly's eyes constricted to hear her full name, which told Hope that it had probably been a term of endearment used by one or both of her parents. Possibly Ethan, too. "I care a great deal about what happens to you, and I will stop at nothing to help you."

Now Molly's dark eyes clouded. Mistrust? Doubt?

"And your uncle Ethan loves you more than life itself. You know that's true. Your mom and dad trusted him to care for you because they believed he'd do everything in his power to do what's best for you. He's trying, Molly—trying so very hard. It's breaking his heart seeing you so miserable, not knowing how to comfort you...."

Molly blinked once, twice, then looked over at the window.

But Hope had meant what she'd said. She had no intention of giving up on this kid. Gently, she cupped Molly's chin in one palm until they sat eye to eye. "Tell me why you've been breaking things. Or why you haven't been eating. Or why you refuse to talk."

To this point, it had been Hope's job to establish trust, to get the girl accustomed to questions, even if none garnered an answer. Until now, she'd been busy building the bridge that would take her across the chasm Molly had constructed to separate her from human companionship and comfort, from reminders of her stable, loving past.

Well, the foundation had been laid, and now the time had come to complete construction on that bridge, word by word. "You're very angry with them, aren't you?"

Molly's eyes widened.

"You're *so* mad at your mom and dad, you're just speechless, aren't you!"

Molly shook her head as her eyes misted with tears.

"It's okay to be angry, sweetie. It's okay...and it's perfectly normal to be furious with them for putting themselves in danger that night."

Fat tears rolled down Molly's cheeks and plopped into her upturned palms.

"You believe if they had loved you more, they might have done something differently to prevent the accident. But they didn't, did they? And so you feel as though they let you down."

This time, when she shook her head, Molly's face was concealed by a veil of dark hair. She'd spoken only one line in all this time, but the words and the tears were proof Hope was getting through to her. Getting on her knees, Hope wrapped her arms around the child. "Oh, Molly, Molly, Molly," she chanted, struggling to stanch her own tears. "Don't punish yourself any more, sweetie. It wasn't your fault!"

Their gazes fused for several tense moments—Hope was intent on sending the message through her eyes that she would not give up, would *not* let up; Molly's eyes said the opposite. Her hands trembled. Her lips quivered. And with one heartrending cry, she wrapped her arms around Hope and began to sob.

"Oh, honey," Hope said, kissing her tear-dampened cheeks, "you're gonna be all right. Everything will be all right, I promise. We'll get to the bottom of this if it takes all night and—"

The door to Ethan's office banged open to reveal him standing there, fists clenched at his sides. "What's going on in here?"

Hope didn't need to turn and look at him to know how furious he was. What she didn't know was *why*.

He crossed the room in three long strides, wrenched Molly from Hope's arms, and wrapped her in a protective hug. "What's the meaning of this?" he demanded. "I hired you to help her, not hurt her!"

"Ethan," she began, surprised at the timidity in her voice, "you don't understand. Molly and I—"

"It's okay, sweet girl," he crooned, "it's all right. Uncle Ethan is here now...."

Despite his tender ministrations, Molly continued to cry... into Ethan's shoulder now.

Hope got to her feet and paced the plush Persian carpet in front of his desk. "Don't do this, Ethan," she said, stopping beside him. "If you usurp my authority this way, you'll—"

Holding Molly as if she were a toddler, he stared her down. "Usurp your authority? Let me remind you that you're in *my* house, Miss Majors, for one reason and one reason only: to help Molly." He hugged the girl tighter. "And from the looks of things, you're doing anything *but* that."

"Believe it or not, there was a purpose to my—"

"You're right. I don't believe it. I have no idea how the parents of your other patients behave at times like this, but I will not stand idly by while you torture *my* kid. She's been through enough. What she needs is—"

"What she needs," Hope said, slowly, deliberately, "is a guardian who will—"

"I'm not just her guardian!" he thundered. "Sam and Shari wanted me to be her father, and I want that, too!"

"Then act like one." She gave him a moment to react, then aimed a forefinger at him. "You need to leave Molly and me alone to continue our work. I know it isn't easy listening to her eternal silence, watching her cry, but...." She swallowed, praying that the Lord would help her find the right words—words that would console him while also comforting Molly. "You told me I was chosen from hundreds of therapists because of my success with kids like Molly."

He looked from her to Molly and back again.

"I know better than anyone that you want to do what's in her best interests. So trust me, Ethan." She laid a hand on his forearm and whispered, "Okay?"

She'd expected his angry expression to relax. Expected him to put Molly back in her chair. To stumble through a halfhearted apology and agree to leave her alone with the child to continue the session.

But none of that happened. In fact, she wouldn't have been at all surprised to hear him insist that she leave, right away, and never come back.

"I wish I could tell you this would all be over soon, Ethan; that it would be easy to reach a satisfying end. But I've been up-front with you so far, and I see no reason to be anything but honest with you now. I know what works. So you're just going to have to put some faith in—"

"Hold it right there," he barked. "Bullying my girl was never part of the plan. If I'd known browbeating and intimidation would be part of your therapy, I'd never have consented to—"

Hope gasped, cutting him off. "I know what it looked like, but you have to believe me, it—"

"Stop it!" Molly cried, clamping her hands over her ears and shaking her head. "Stop it right now!"

Ethan set her on her feet and got on one knee. Tears pooled in his eyes as he cradled her face with both hands. "Molly, darlin'!" he said, his voice gravelly with emotion, "you...you *talked*!" Pulling her close, he shut his eyes.

A moment later, he looked up at Hope. "She talked," he said, stunned. "Molly *talked*."

The argument, the accusations, the anger vanished as he and Hope both wrapped Molly in an embrace, their arms overlapping around her. Ethan linked his fingers with Hope's and gave a gentle squeeze. "Sorry," he managed to say around a sob. "I didn't know. I didn't realize...."

Hope was optimistic but guarded. She'd been down this road enough times to know that what had just happened was nothing to pin their hopes on. Molly's exclamation could have been a sign that she was close to recovery, but it just as easily could have been a fluke, a momentary flare-up, induced by the emotionally charged atmosphere in the room.

Although it went against everything she'd learned about psychological disorders and their treatments, about disappointments and expectations, she went ahead and hoped, anyway.

Chapter Ten

Hope had been letting him off the hook for far too long.

As she backed out of the parking space in front of her office building, she thought of the many occasions when Ethan had willingly participated in counseling sessions with Molly. Rearranging his overcrowded calendar had often required some fancy footwork, but he'd done it, quickly and without complaint. She drove toward his house, her mind abuzz with conflicting thoughts. He was a man to be reckoned with, to be sure. But did he really expect her to believe he was influential enough to put the governor on hold for Molly yet couldn't get out of an appointment in order to meet alone with Hope? *What's he afraid of?* she wondered.

Over the years, Hope had learned that a client's face—his facial expressions, his fleeting smiles or sneers—told nearly as much as the words he said. And if the stark look of dread on Ethan's face each time she suggested a one-on-one between them wasn't fear, she had no idea how to define it.

She recalled the article she'd read that claimed dentists are three times more likely than other professionals to commit suicide because they spend so much time looking into the eyes of fear. But frustration at not being able to help their patients surely put psychiatrists in a position of even greater likelihood of suicide. Hope shook her head. *I have three strikes against me without even trying,* she thought. Her mother had killed herself, she'd chosen psychiatry as a profession, and she spent her days drilling patients for information. *Thank God I have the Lord on my side!*

And she'd stay close to Him in the weeks to come....

She'd met Ethan in early fall, when the trees along the Baltimore Beltway were still green and full of leaves. Nearly two months had passed since then, and with each passing week, driving back and forth on I-695 between Rockville and Potomac, Hope had witnessed the subtle seasonal changes in nature. Now, the once-verdant trees glowed with blazing orange and burnt yellow.

But seasons past had taught her that the beauty of autumn is deceptive, for it is but a harbinger of winter's unwavering approach. In a little while, the limbs that now gleamed gold and scarlet would be stripped bare by blustery gusts, and, before long, the bright blue sky would dim to pale gray as the wind's frosty breath blew fall's cottony clouds to the far corners of the planet.

Ethan reminded her a bit of the wind—warm and soothing one day, cold and unnerving the next.

"We've been putting this off for days," she'd said on the phone that morning. "For Molly's sake, we need to talk today...alone."

And he hadn't minced words. "Then for Molly's sake, let's do it."

His emphasis on "for Molly's sake" showed how drastically their relationship had cooled since the argument. During their conversation, she had heard him popping the locks on his brief-case, rifling through its contents in search of his BlackBerry. "Tomorrow, six o'clock? Maria won't mind staying late just this once."

"She's a wonderful woman," Hope had said. "No need to put her to that trouble. I'll be there for my regular session with Molly at seven. Maybe we can talk after she's gone to bed instead."

"See you then," he'd said before hanging up.

Hope sighed heavily. "Help me, Lord. I'm at my wit's end. Please tell me what to do...for both of them."

As she neared the big house on the Potomac, her mind drifted to the articles she'd read about the self-made millionaire. One article in particular—"Nice Guys Finish First"—stuck out in her mind. "Like any other predator," Earl Shores had written, "Burke is cunning and stealthy, and patient enough to scope out the horizon in search of the young, the ailing, and the weak." Shores had filled an entire sidebar with the names of company presidents and corporations that had "fallen prey" to Ethan's incredible skills as a hunter. The facts, as presented by the reporter, made the headline all the more ironic, considering all that Ethan had done for his godchild.

Maybe when all this was over, once she'd put Molly on the path to healing and things were right between her and Ethan, Hope would take a much-needed vacation. She'd always loved the shore with its shell-strewn beaches and screeching seagulls. The quiet would be healing for *her* at this time of year, without scores of sunbathers hogging the beach and noisy children running around and splashing in the water. Long walks at the edge of the chilly surf soothed and calmed her as few things could...if she was careful not to wade out too far. She never had learned to swim.

She thought of Molly. Of Ethan. Of how very much she'd come to care for them both. And she prayed she wasn't in over her head.

❦

Maria had worked for Ethan for years and, even during her first week on the job, had never been the least bit shy about asking for—or telling him—what she needed. So the faint knock at the door of his study and the timid expression on her face when he told her to come in surprised him enough to say, "Maria, you—you look like you've seen a ghost!"

She looked furtively over one shoulder. "You have…you have company, Meester Burke." She pointed. "Downstairs, in the billiards room."

"Company?" The art deco grandfather clock behind her read 5:15. The only visitor he was expecting was Hope, but not until 7:00. Had she changed her mind about talking with him after her session with Molly? With more than a little impatience, he strode toward the door and caught a glimpse out the front window. "What are all those cars doing on the front lawn?" he asked Maria. "There must be thirty or forty—"

"Ethan!" said a sultry voice from behind him. "Happy birthday."

As he turned, Kate pressed a lingering kiss to the corner of his mouth.

"Kate," he said, placing his hands on her shoulders to keep her from getting any closer. "What are you doing here?" After the episode when Ethan had written Hope's name over and over on his notepad, Kate had turned up the heat in an even greater attempt to attract his attention. She'd stayed within the bounds of professional office propriety, yet she'd managed to let him know she had no intention of giving up without a fight.

She inclined her bleach-blonde head and smiled seductively. "Why, I've brought you a birthday present," she said breathily.

Ethan looked past her at Maria, who shrugged and held out both hands. "Don't look at me," she said. "I just work here."

Kate grabbed his arm and led him down the hall. "I'd blindfold you," she said, laughing as they reached the stairs, "but I've never been very good with knots. Besides, you could fall down—"

"Kate," he said, wriggling free of her grasp, "what's with all the cars out there?"

She kissed him again, this time on the lips. "It's a party, silly! You haven't done anything fun in months. What better excuse to kick up your heels than a birthday celebration?"

He took a deep breath, hoping it might help him summon the patience to keep from booting her out the front door. What made her think she could waltz into his home, uninvited, and behave like the lady of the manor?

It was clear he needed to stop focusing all his extra attention on Molly. And Hope. The distraction had allowed Kate to move in way too close. She was an excellent marketing manager, period. The time had come to make sure she understood they would never be more than employer and employee. "Kate," he growled, "you're overstepping your—"

"There he is!" someone shouted from downstairs. "Look, everybody, the birthday boy is here!"

Cheers bubbled up the steps as his employees gathered in the foyer. "C'mon down," someone said, and Kate added, "There's pâté and truffles and the most marvelous jellied mousse. All your favorites!" She leaned close to whisper into his ear, "And...some very special *presents*."

Frowning, he looked into her heavily made-up eyes. "Who told you it was my birthday?"

She'd always seemed so poised, so sure of herself, but under his scathing, demanding stare, Kate blinked and, for the first time since he'd met her, seemed uncertain what to do next.

She opted for humor. "I didn't realize your birthday was a corporate secret," she said, laughing. "Isn't this what you pay me for? To publicize you and Burke Enterprises?"

He hadn't noticed the TV cameras until that moment. Gritting his teeth, Ethan said, "Of all the...."

"Smile, Ethan," hollered a cameraman.

"We're live for the six o'clock news," said the reporter.

The media had never felt the need to stand on ceremony with him. He'd never been "Mr. Burke," because he'd encouraged the down-to-earth, friendly persona. Plastering a smile on his face, he slid an arm around Kate's shoulders. "Do you believe the gall of this woman, barging in here like she owns the place to throw me a birthday party?"

Amid the applause and laughter, Kate chose that moment to kiss his cheek.

"See if anyone needs a drink or some food," he said, stepping back. And to the reporter, he said, "I'll be down in just a second." He wiggled his eyebrows. "Few loose ends to tie up. Use the time to see what juicy gossip you can wrangle from my employees."

Maria was still standing behind him, looking confused and upset. "I did not know, Meester Burke. I open thee door, and Meese Kate, she shove right inside. I—"

"I know," he said, giving her shoulder a reassuring squeeze. "Bet now you wish you'd taken that class in night school...."

"Wheech class?"

"How to Avoid a Steamroller," he said, winking.

"They made a movie about theese one," she said. "I theenk it was called *Godzilla*."

Ethan laughed as the doorbell rang. "Tell whomever it is that we're at maximum capacity. I don't need the fire marshal breathing down my neck."

Kate opened the door as if on cue and ushered a caterer inside. Behind him was a group of black-suited young men and women carrying trays with white doilies into the kitchen.

"You theenk maybe Molly, she would like to join the party?"

He shrugged, wondering what Hope would recommend. "Don't suppose it could hurt any. If she wants to come down, it's fine with me," he said, heading back into his study. "I'll be only a few minutes," he added, closing the door.

With a glance at his Rolex, Ethan realized Hope would arrive in a little over an hour. And the party would be going full tilt by then. How would she feel about walking in on a birthday bash?

He got a picture of her face, wide-eyed with disbelief, and wondered how long it would take her to say, "We'll reschedule our session for a more convenient time...."

If she hadn't been there dozens of times, Hope might have thought she'd made a wrong turn somewhere. Why were a Channel Two van and a WQSR radio station car parked among dozens of others on his neatly mowed lawn?

The housekeeper threw open the door even before Hope could ring the bell. "Meese Majors," she said, hugging her. "I'm so glad you are here!" Looking toward the heavens, she raised her arms, then let them drop to her sides. "Meester Burke, he will need you. That *Kate* woman...ay-ay-ay-ay," she said, shaking her head.

Hope had never seen the spunky woman without a cheery smile on her broad face. "What's wrong, Maria?"

The unmistakable sounds of merriment filtered up from the lower level of the house. Voices engaged in laughter and conversation harmonized with the tinkling of ice cubes, the clang of flatware connecting with china, and the barely audible melody of music coming from the sound system. Maria closed the front door behind them. "You be careful of that one, Meese Majors," she whispered.

Hope swallowed a lump of nervousness without even knowing why she felt anxious. "Be careful? Why would I need to—?"

"That one, she eees trouble, I tell you." With one finger in the air, the woman said, "I am not at leeeberty to say more, but... please be careful, *si?*" With that, she disappeared into the kitchen.

Hope couldn't help but wonder why Ethan hadn't told her about the party. If he didn't want her here, surely he'd have come up with some excuse to postpone their session. She glanced toward the stairs, wondering where Molly was. Maybe—

"Well, well, well. What do we have here?" said a saucy female voice.

Hope turned as the woman thrust a limp, red-clawed hand in her direction. "How rude of me. I'm Kate, and I, um, *work* for Ethan...?"

Her emphasis on the word *work* hadn't been accidental, and Hope was left wondering why Ethan had never mentioned the woman.

"It's his birthday, you know," Kate continued.

"Oh. I—I didn't realize. I—we have.... I'm Hope Majors, Molly's counselor."

It made no sense to Hope why Kate's eyes narrowed at the mention of her name. Made no sense that her voice took on an icy edge when she said, "Ethan is terribly busy, I'm afraid, so perhaps you can come back some other time, when—"

"Of course," Hope said. "He must have forgotten about the party when he scheduled the appointment. Perhaps you'll be kind enough to let him know I was here?" But even as the words passed her lips, Hope knew Ethan would never hear from Kate that she'd stopped by. She headed for the stairs, intent on stopping in Molly's room. "I'll just get to work with Molly, and—"

Kate bit her lower lip, then said, "Oh, dear…he hasn't told you, then?"

Fear pounded in her heart. She had one foot on the first step, the other on the foyer floor, when she asked, "Told me what?"

The big blonde looked around as if checking for eavesdroppers. "I hate to be the one to break this to you," she said, "but I happen to know that Ethan has been interviewing other therapists."

How could Kate know such a thing unless Ethan had told her himself?

"Men!" Kate said, shaking her head. "They can be so self-centered. How rude of him not to call you. He could have saved you the trip over here." Stepping aside, she opened the front door. "When he gets to the office tomorrow, I'll be sure he calls you, first thing. He owes you a big apology!"

Hope remembered Maria's warning. "He doesn't owe me anything," she said, digging through her purse. "Least of all an apology!" Jangling her car keys, Hope smiled. "Nice meeting you," she said as Kate leaned on the doorjamb, one high-heeled foot crossed over the other.

When she was halfway to her car, Ethan's voice stopped her. "Hey, Hope! Where are you going?"

She turned, heartened by his warm, welcoming smile. But her feelings of elation died an immediate death when she noticed the unmistakable splotches of lipstick on his cheeks, on his lips…lipstick the same shade of red as Kate's….

Hope had admitted her feelings for Ethan to herself, but until that moment, she hadn't realized just how much she'd come to care for him. Seeing evidence that he and Kate had a relationship that was obviously more than professional—well, it made things painfully clear. That kiss? The warm hugs? She didn't understand what they'd meant, but she understood the possessive way Kate linked her arm through his.

Turning on her heel, Hope hurried to her car. She didn't bother to buckle her seatbelt or check her mirrors, and as she backed onto his circular driveway, she knew that it was by the grace of God she didn't collide with another car.

If she'd received Maria's message earlier, maybe she'd have been spared this humiliation.

Correction, she thought, fighting tears. *Heartache*.

Chapter Eleven

H ope!" Ethan hollered as she sped off. "Hope, wait up!"

He took a shortcut, high-jumping a boxwood hedge and zigzagging across the lawn in an attempt to cut her off farther down the drive. "Hope, for cryin' out loud, will you *wait!*" Whether she didn't hear him or was choosing to ignore him, Ethan didn't know. He understood only that she was bound and determined to get off his property as fast as possible.

Kate was waiting for him when he returned to the foyer. "What was that all about?" he demanded, slamming the door.

"I have no idea," she said, shrugging innocently. "I came up to check on the caterers and saw her at the bottom of the stairs. Guess she took it wrong when I said you and Molly were busy with the party and your guests."

Oh, she was good, real good. But Ethan was practiced at detecting guile, and he had dozens of corporate takeovers under his belt to prove it. Kate was attractive enough—if you liked girls big and blonde and pushy—and a year or so ago, he probably would have said she was just his type. But that was before he realized how much more he preferred a petite woman with freckles and green eyes, fiery red curls, and a smile that would melt the ice in his sarsaparilla.

He caught a glimpse of himself in the hall mirror behind Kate's head and saw the lipstick blotches around his mouth—Kate's not-so-subtle "brand." No doubt Hope had seem them, too. Had she run off like a scared rabbit because she'd been jealous?

The idea made him smile a bit.

But the moment didn't last long, because Kate reached out to tidy his collar with a haughty "I'm-too-sexy-for-my-party-dress" grin on her face.

Ethan didn't understand how Kate had known precisely when Hope would arrive, but he had no doubt that she'd timed the party to coincide with Molly's session. She'd never thrown a party for him before, so why now, after nearly five years' employment with him? It was a clever ruse, he decided, that allowed her to communicate her intentions. And, sadly, Hope had read the message loud and clear.

Kate's attitude might have made sense if he'd given her a sign that he was interested in her. How ever had she gotten the notion that they were more than employer and employee?

"What's going on inside that handsome head of yours?" Kate asked, sidling up to him.

He felt another caress coming his way and barred it with his forearm. "Trust me, Kate, you do not want me to answer that question."

"But of course I do, darling," she cooed, combing her long, painted fingernails through his hair. "You *know* I do!"

Despite his best efforts to prevent her, she managed to press herself against his side, so he put his hands on her shoulders and gave her a gentle shake. "That woman you just chased away?"

Kate read the wrong message from his hands-on approach and rested her hands on his shoulders. "Adorable little thing. Molly's counselor, right?"

"Adorable. Yes. Most adorable woman I've ever laid eyes on."

Her self-assured smirk faded.

"She's smart and talented, too, and sweet as cotton candy...."

Blinking, Kate took a small step back.

But Ethan was merely warming up. "With a smile brighter than the sun and eyes a man could get lost in, the voice of an angel, and—"

Giggling nervously, Kate licked her lips. "Ethan, *darling*, you'd better be careful, or people will get the idea you're—"

"That I'm in love with her?" One corner of his mouth lifted in a grin.

And Kate's blue eyes narrowed.

"I have to hand it to you, Kate."

She swallowed. "W-what?"

"Well, I knew pretty much from the get-go that I liked her, but until today, I never realized how *much*." He gave her a light kiss right in the middle of her forehead. "So thanks, kiddo, for helping me see what's been right under my nose all along."

"B-but Ethan," she stammered, "I thought, I—"

"I know," he said, turning her toward the door that led to the party downstairs, "you never expected that playing cupid would be part of your job description, did you?"

She stood alone on the landing, arms hanging limp at her sides.

"I believe in repaying deeds in kind," he said evenly, giving her a moment to mull over his meaning. "You'll find the best letter of recommendation you've ever read in your pay envelope next week and a big fat severance check, too."

Kate gasped as all ten fingers fluttered near her throat. "Recommendation? Severance? Ethan, surely you can't mean—"

He held up an index finger, commanding her silence. "I can, *darling*, and I do." Shrugging, he added, "It's one of the perks about bein' the boss." His stern expression was matched by the angry rasp of his voice. "I don't have to work with people I don't trust."

"But when you hired me, you said I was one of the best marketers in the business. It's what you said when you gave me my last raise, and—"

"Your work for Burke Enterprises has been impeccable," he said, cutting her off. "But you can't seem to grasp the boundaries of your job. Now, why not go downstairs, cut yourself a big piece of the birthday cake I probably paid too much for, and enjoy the party you threw to help me celebrate the fact I've finally come to my senses…about a lot of things."

As he turned to go downstairs, she said, "They're right about you. You *are* heartless!"

Ethan stopped dead in his tracks, made a slow pivot, and looked her right in the eyes. "The word is 'ruthless,' *darling*, and I earned it by knowing whom I can—and can't—trust."

⁂

Hope was going to wear a path in the carpet if she didn't stop pacing back and forth across her living room. *I behaved like a little ninny—a jealous little ninny!* was her mental self-castigation.

She had come so close to making a breakthrough with Molly, and now her unprofessionalism was threatening to blow everything up. It would be a miracle if Ethan allowed her to spend another moment with his girl!

What must he think of her, running off as though she had a pit bull on her heels? Hope got a quick mental picture of his face, spotted here and there with the imprints of Kate's kisses, and her stomach twisted into a knot.

Several times, she'd come close to admitting out loud that her feelings for him ran deep. But each time, she'd reined in her emotions. Excused them. Rationalized them. Pretended they were nothing more than the natural consequences of a schoolgirl crush...the direct result of too many years spent dreaming that someday, a white knight would carry her off to a rose-covered cottage.

She knew what she had to do.

But first, a little sustenance....

Hope fell to her knees right there in the middle of the living room, bowed her head, and folded her hands. With eyes closed, she prayed aloud. "Dear Lord, give me the courage to face my fears and own up to my mistakes. Open my heart and mind to accept Your wisdom and guidance, so I'll know what to say when I see...." Her heart pounded with dread at the mere thought of facing him. "...When I see him again."

The last thing she wanted to do was to get into her car, drive down that dark and deserted road to his riverfront home, and admit what a fool she'd been—and how horribly it would impact poor, innocent little Molly. But it was the right thing to do.

Hope had to convince Ethan to give her another chance, because she was close, so close, to reaching Molly. She'd give him much assurance to convince him to let her finish what she'd started.

"Almighty Father, bless me with the grace to do what's best for both of them, because I...."

Opening her eyes, she held her breath as the truth crashed around her like waves on the shore. "I love her," she whispered. "God help me, I love that little girl!"

She'd violated just about every rule of professional decorum ever written, but Hope knew she couldn't blame it all on her feelings for Molly. Admittedly, the child's history and her own were similar, but the real source of her departure from professional behavior was rooted in how she felt about Ethan.

Tears sprang to her eyes as she admitted, "Lord help me, I love him, too…." Then, on the heels of a shuddering sigh, Hope prayed, "Put my mind right, Lord. Help me focus on the important things in life, like obeying Your Word and helping *all* my patients find solace."

A sense of peace engulfed her, and she believed she would find the strength to do the right thing, for the right reasons. On her feet now, she crossed to the stereo and popped in a CD, letting the soothing, Spirit-filled music bring her an even greater calm. She decided to do something with her hair, repair the damage her tears had done to her makeup, and then change into something comfortable before heading back to Ethan's. It was a weeknight, after all, and the partygoers had to work the next morning. Surely, they would be gone by the time she got there.

The drive to the river seemed to take far less time than the usual twenty minutes, partly because she recited the Twenty-third Psalm the entire way.

It wouldn't be easy.

But she'd do it.

Maybe, by the time she arrived at his house, she would actually believe that.

⤬

Ethan knocked softly on Molly's door. "Hey, sweetie," he called, "mind if I come in?"

No response…par for the course. So, he turned the knob and slowly peeked into the room.

She wasn't at her desk or on the window seat, nor in the closet or the bathroom. Puzzled, he headed back down the hall to find

Maria. The woman never missed a thing. Surely, she'd know where the girl had gone.

He found his housekeeper in the kitchen, loading the dishwasher. "You should have left hours ago," he admitted.

"And leave you weeth theese mess? Not me, Meester Burke," she said, laughing.

"I don't know what I ever did to deserve you. You're the best." Then, "You haven't seen Molly, have you?"

"Eeen her favorite place. Where else?"

Ethan grabbed his jacket from the wooden peg behind the door and headed outside. Pocketing his hands, he walked down the gentle slope of lawn toward the riverbank and soon heard the unmistakable *plink-plunk* of pebbles plopping into the murky water. Molly came into view, sitting on the pier with her bare toes dangling in the water.

"Kinda cold to be doin' that, don't you think?"

When she didn't answer, he hunkered down beside her. "So, what brought you out here in the dark, all by yourself?"

She shrugged.

If he'd asked her that before Sam and Shari died, she might have said, "I'm not alone. God is up there in the sky, with the stars and the moon; there are birds roosting in the trees...and there's you."

He made a move to sling an arm over her shoulders when he noticed the duffle bag stuffed to overflowing beside her. "Hey, what's this?"

Another shrug.

"Planning to run away from home, are you?"

Molly sighed.

Ethan pretended his heart wasn't aching with dread. If he hadn't come out here when he had, would she have gone? Ethan cleared his throat and put his fear into words. "How far do you think you could go...li'l gal who refuses to talk?"

Silence.

"Well, I hope you packed money. Plenty of it."

She nodded.

"Good, good, 'cause a girl needs money when she's on the run."

More silence.

"Might be kinda hard, though, going into a diner, trying to get a meal...."

She turned slightly.

"I mean, what're you planning to do, point at the menu to order?"

Molly blinked and tucked in one corner of her mouth.

"Ahh, I see," he said, nodding. "You hadn't thought it through that far, right?"

She shook her head.

"Then I wonder if you gave any thought to where you'd sleep. It's November. Gets pretty cold, 'specially at night, y'know...."

Her shoulders slumped.

"Hmm...hadn't thought of that, either, I take it...."

She shook her head again.

"Well, I know that a smart kid like you would have taken the time to think things through...if something hadn't distracted her. Was it that awful, noisy party?"

One shoulder rose in a half-shrug, and Ethan got to his feet. "Tell you what," he said. "Put your shoes on, and we'll head inside.

Maria hasn't left yet, so maybe we can talk her into whipping us up a pot of her famous hot cocoa, and some of that amazing popcorn...."

When Molly looked up at him, the stars glinted in her dark eyes. He wanted to gather her close, hug her tight, and promise her the world would right itself soon. But like he'd said...she was a smart kid. No way she'd believe it, especially after all she'd been through lately.

Ethan settled for the feel of her warm little hand tucked into his big one. Side by side, they walked across the decking at the end of his yard. They'd just passed the gazebo when she blurted out, "My suitcase!"

A sob ached in his throat at the sound of her voice, hoarse and craggy from lack of use. But he bit his tongue and thanked God silently as she ran back to fetch the duffle. When she caught up to him again, he took it from her and dropped it on the lawn. "Remember how we used to sit in the gazebo for hours, just watching and listening for critters?"

Smiling, she nodded.

"What do you think...in the mood to do that now?"

Smiling wider, she nodded again.

He carried the bag inside as she settled on the bench facing the river, then came back out and sat down beside her, drawing her close in a sideways hug. Almost instantly, she rested her head on his shoulder.

"Last week," he whispered, "I saw a deer, right there in the woods." He pointed at the spot. "Big, burly buck with antlers as wide as this gazebo!"

"Hmpf," she said, grinning suspiciously. But he noticed that she'd immediately begun scanning the tree line for a glimpse of the big deer. "Uncle Ethan?"

It startled him more than he cared to admit, hearing her soft whisper so near to his ear. "What, sweetie?" he whispered back.

She pointed, and he followed her gaze to a spot beyond the brush where three does, their white tails flicking like warning flags, stood looking straight back at them. "How many?" he asked, hoping to coax more conversation from her.

"Just three…."

"Just three," he echoed, wishing Hope were there to share the joyous moment.

Chapter Twelve

Following the directions Maria had given her, Hope headed down the path leading to the Potomac. She'd expected to hear Ethan's voice by the time her sneakers hit the weathered wood decking or to see Molly and Ethan, silhouetted by the moonlit sky. Had the housekeeper been mistaken? Maybe Molly hadn't headed for her favorite spot at her uncle Ethan's house after all....

Just then, his manly baritone floated toward her on the crisp November air. "I love you, sweet girl," she heard him say. She stopped walking, trying to pinpoint the direction from which his voice had come.

"You know that, don't you?"

The gazebo, she realized, but she saw no reason to move closer. Standing under the umbrella of the bare-branched willow was a bit like being in her own private auditorium.

"That bag you packed," he was saying, "is pretty heavy."

Hope read the silence to mean that Molly hadn't answered.

"Felt pretty good, didn't it," he continued, "when you got some help lugging it back up the walk?"

Hope took a step forward, which enabled her to see the shadowy figures of Ethan and Molly, huddled together in the darkness. When Molly nodded, Hope saw Ethan close his eyes and look up as if thanking God for the response, however silent.

"How much do you know about Miss Majors?" Ethan said next.

The blood froze in Hope's veins.

"Did you know she's an orphan, just like you?"

Molly turned on the bench to face him.

"She hasn't had a mom or a dad since she was a baby. Her aunt and uncle raised her." He kissed Molly's forehead. "Gotta admire somebody like that...."

Tears welled in Hope's eyes, and a sob ached in her throat. Had she misread the scene earlier between him and Kate?

"It's my fault," Molly said.

And Ethan asked, "What's your fault?"

"Mom and Dad...the...the accident...it was my fault."

Hope tensed, wondering what he'd say or do, wondering if she ought to join them.

"Why would you say such a thing?" Ethan asked.

"Because. It's true."

He gathered her closer and lifted her chin with his forefinger. "How 'bout explaining it to your poor old uncle Ethan...."

"I was at Sally's house that night. I was supposed to stay till morning." She sighed. "But Sally and me had a fight and I wanted to go home. So I called them, told them to come get me."

"Nothing wrong with that," Ethan interjected.

"But Mom said Dad had just got home, that he was extra tired. And I knew she never learned how to drive that new car, but I didn't care. I wanted to go home."

For a while, neither of them spoke. Hope was formulating in her mind how she might handle the situation in his shoes when he said, "Taking the blame for something like that? Well, that's a pretty heavy bag to carry all by yourself."

Molly sniffed.

"Maybe you oughtta let me help you carry it."

Silence.

"...Like you let me help you carry your suitcase."

More silence.

"You packed that thing pretty full...."

The only sound was the water, gently slapping the shore.

"It was nice, wasn't it, having help?"

"Yes...."

"So, what do you say, Molly-girl? Will you let me help you with this one, too?"

The wind rustled through the underbrush. *It's what angels' wings must sound like,* Hope thought, watching the answer to a prayer unfold before her eyes. As a girl, the thought had calmed her when the night wind, soughing past her windows, made her huddle under the sheets, feeling alone and afraid. *The breath of God,* she'd tell herself. And, in no time, her fears would evaporate.

The same serenity enveloped her now. "Be not afraid," Jesus had promised, "for I am with you."

Christ was with Ethan now, too, guiding his every word.

"I aim to help you see it wasn't your fault. Okay?"

Suddenly, Hope felt every bit like the spy she was. She had no right to be here, trespassing on this profound, private moment. Turning, she headed back to the house, where she would hide out in the powder room until her eyes were no longer puffy from crying tears of relief and joy. Then, she'd do what she'd come here to do and apologize to Ethan.

It would be an uphill battle from here, this business of going on without him, alone.

No...not alone. She'd always have the Lord.

Ethan didn't need her. He'd never needed her. Hope knew that now, and the proof had been in his voice, in his words, in every action he'd taken moments ago...and since they'd met.

The inky sky overhead twinkled with the gleam of a million stars, and Hope looked up into the knowing eyes of God, whispering her request....

∞

Ten years later,
in the home of Mr. and Mrs. Ethan Burke

"Molly, would you call your father for me, please?"

The young woman gave her mother a gently playful elbow to the ribs. "Sure, Mom. What would you like me to call him?"

Hope laughed. "Quit fooling around, silly girl. Supper's getting cold!"

Molly's smile was mirrored in her dark eyes. Giggling, she headed for the family room. "But I'm not even hungry yet! It's three hours earlier at Stanford, y'know."

"Well, you can at least sit at the table and visit with us, Miss I'm-Gonna-Be-a-Pediatrician." Hope gave her a sideways hug. It seemed the girl hadn't stopped talking—not even for a minute!—since that night in the gazebo when Ethan had promised to be there for her always, to help her carry her burdens.

Now, Ethan sidled up behind Hope and wrapped his arms around her in an affectionate hug. "Whatcha thinkin', pretty lady?"

She leaned against him. "Oh, just remembering bygone days, that's all."

He turned her to face him. "You don't mean…?"

Blushing, she said, "What?"

"You've been in la-la land for days now. At first, I chalked it up to Molly coming home for the summer. But now I'm not so sure."

Her flush intensified. He'd always known her better than anyone, so it shouldn't have surprised her that he suspected something. She sighed. "I'd hoped to make the announcement over dessert."

He clamped a big hand on each of her shoulders. "Are you saying what I think you're saying?"

"This one's due on Valentine's Day."

Gathering her close, he chuckled into her ear. "Well now, how 'bout that?" He kissed her cheek. "Maybe we ought to name him Cupid."

Hope crinkled her nose.

"Okay, you're right." Stroking his jaw, he gave it a moment's thought. He pointed his forefinger in the air and said, "I've got it! Candy if it's a girl, Valentino for a boy!"

She wrapped her arms around him. "And what if it's twins again?"

"Hmm…you've got me there." After kissing the tip of her nose, he said, "You make me so happy. Repairing the relationship between my dad and me, convincing me that what happened to Bess and my mom wasn't my fault, getting Molly over her emotional hurdles…."

"These have been the best years of my life," Hope said.

"Mine, too." He paused, frowning slightly. "You're not sorry that you gave up counseling? Not even once in a while?"

"Are you kidding? It's all I do around here, breaking up squabbles between the twins! Seriously, look what you've done for *me*:

giving me Sawyer as a substitute father and Maria as a dear friend, putting me in charge of day care at Burke Enterprises, and—"

"Well, just 'cause you're in charge of the program doesn't mean you have to fill every classroom single-handedly!"

"You had a little to do with that, need I remind you?"

He wiggled his eyebrows. "No, m'dear, you never need to remind me of anything so blessedly glorious."

She snuggled closer to him. "God has been very good to us, hasn't He?"

"Sure has." Chuckling, Ethan added, "We've been pretty good to Him, too."

Hope leaned back. "What?"

"Well, the church softball team was four players shy last season, and the Burke family filled every empty seat in the dugout."

Hope shook her head. "I'll make you a deal," she said, one palm pressed to each of his cheeks. "Stop saying sacrilegious things like that and I'll fix your favorite dessert—anytime you want it—for the rest of your life."

"Homemade apple pie, fresh from the oven, with a slab of cheddar cheese on top? For the rest of my *life*? Are you serious…?"

"Serious as a judge."

"Then you've got yourself a deal, baby."

She studied his face and, grinning, said, "Now, why don't I trust you?"

"Maybe because we need to seal this deal with a kiss."

"Oh, you!" she said, laughing. "I love you."

"I love you, too. And I like this system."

"What system?"

"The way we seal every deal with a kiss. Now, close your eyes and pucker up, lady, 'cause I'm about to plant one on ya!"

About the Author

A prolific writer, Loree Lough has more than seventy books, sixty short stories, and 2,500 articles in print. Her stories have earned dozens of industry and Reader's Choice awards. A frequent guest speaker for writers' organizations, book clubs, private and government institutions, corporations, college and high school writing programs, and more, Loree has encouraged thousands with her comedic approach to "learned-the-hard-way" lessons about the craft and industry.

For decades, Loree has been an avid wolf enthusiast, and she dedicates a portion of her income each year to efforts that benefit the magnificent animals. She splits her time between a home in the Baltimore suburbs and a cabin in the Allegheny Mountains. She shares her life and residences with a spoiled pointer named Cash and her patient, dedicated husband, Larry, who has supported her writing and teaching endeavors throughout the years.

Loree loves hearing from her readers, so feel free to write her at loree@loreelough.com. To learn more about Loree and her books, visit her Web site at www.loreelough.com.